P9-DJU-524

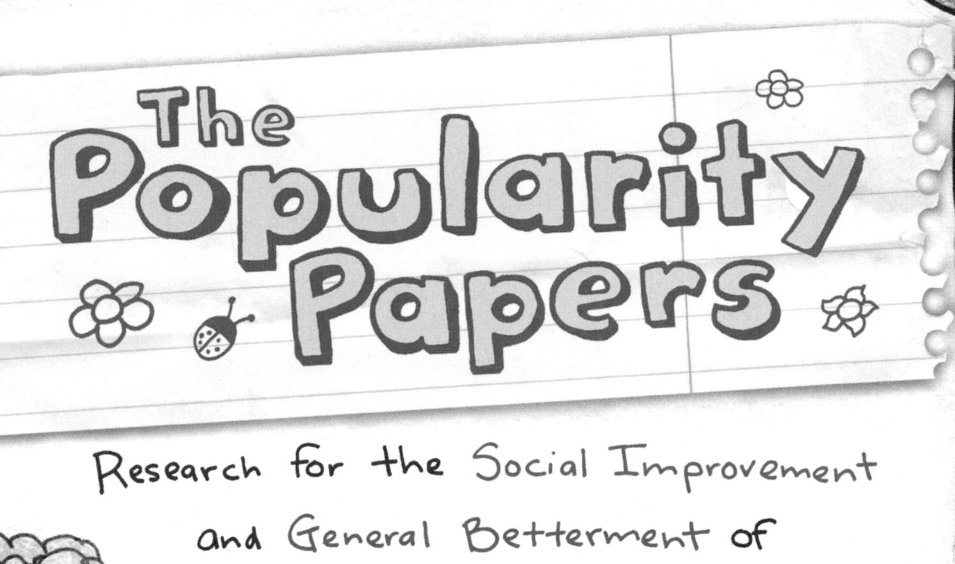

Research for the Social Improvement and General Betterment of

Lydia Goldblatt & Julie Graham-Chang

Amy Ignatow

Amulet Books
New York

Did you get the book?

I did, but I left it at home.

That's ok, we can just paste our notes into it after school.

Like a scrapbook! And I can put my drawings in it too.

Can you draw a picture of Melody?

everything sucks.
I'm Melody

I tried to draw a skull earring but it got all smudgy.

Ha ha ha! It's perfect!!!

The POPULARITY PAPERS

Research for the Social Improvement and General Betterment of

Lydia Goldblatt + Julie Graham-Chang

The authors of
The Popularity Papers
do solemnly swear to never ever
let Outside Eyes (other people)
see the contents of The Popularity
Papers, and that the information
in The Popularity Papers will
only be used so that we
can improve upon ourselves.

x Lydia Goldblatt x Julie Graham-Chang

Editor-in-Chief
Co-Author
Lead Experimenter
Dictator

Associate Editor
Co-Author
Illustrator
Recorder

The Research Team

LYDIA

Lives with Mom and one weird sister

Taller

Blond

I have to wear glasses

I am a really good singer

I wish I had more Style

I love ice Cream

JULIE

Lives with my dads and one bad cat

Not so tall

Brown hair

You can call yourself a Brunette

Okay, Brunette

I'm mostly good at drawing but not so good at drawing cars.

I wish I could fly.

THE very brilliant PLAN

We (Lydia Goldblatt and Julie Graham-Chang) have one whole year before we start Junior High. Based on our observations of Melody (my older sister) a lot can change between elementary school and Junior High.

So our plan (which is very brilliant) is to observe the girls who are already popular. We'll ~~write down~~ record our observations in this book.

Then, when we have enough information about the popular girls, we'll know what it is that they do to be popular and we'll try to do the same things to see if we become popular as well.

Julie (me) is a better artist with clearer handwriting, so I will do most of the recording. Lydia is braver (I am!), so she will put herself into the experiments. For instance, if Julie and Lydia observe that the popular girls all wear the same kind of clothing, then Lydia will be the one to wear said article of clothing to see if it helps to improve her social standing. If, however, Julie and Lydia observe that the Popular Girls all eat a certain type of ice cream, Julie might join in the experimentation (unless the observed ice cream has strawberries in it, which make Julie break out in hives).

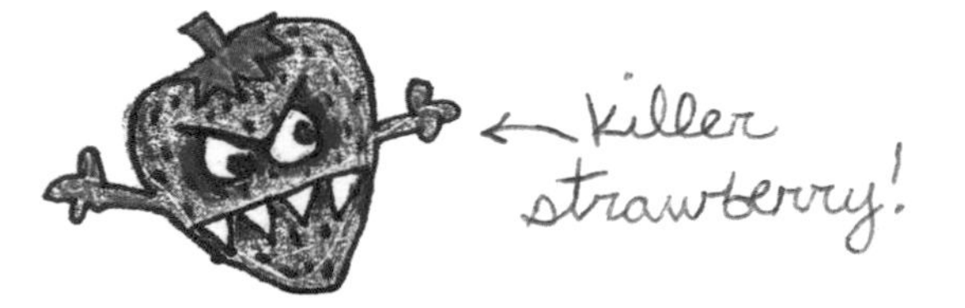

Hopefully, if we are successful in our research and experiments, we will achieve

which are

1. To become popular
2. To never, ever turn into

Melody!!!

3. To stop being referred to as "Goldbladder"

Seriously, I am so sick of that!

Maybe Mike Cavelleri just wants to be your friend because he thinks you pee gold.

Eww!!!

Imagine the money you could make!

Gross!!

REASONS WHY BEING POPULAR is BETTER
(than not being popular)
1. More people like you.
2. Not being teased.
3. When something cool happens (like a pool party) you get to go.
4. Other people want to be you.
5. You get better parts in school plays
6. You are just better.
horribly unpopular!
Popular

September

We should come up with a Code Name for our project.

Cool. How about "The Popularity Project"?

Too obvious. It's a secret study.

Okay. How about "Research Project"?

This is me, dead from boredom.

I'm sooooo sorry. Do you have any ideas?

I can't think right now because you killed me with boredom (see above picture). Let's brainstorm after school.

Will you be alive by then?

Probably.

Ideas for Code Names for our Secret Research Project

- The Fine Fellowship
- Project X
- Project Y (not)
- Method and Result
- The Inquiring Minds

Thesaurus results for "research": inquest, inquiry, inquisition, investigation, probe

I already suggested "Inquiring."

We asked my daddy for suggestions of good names for a secret club, and he said

and we didn't know what he meant, so we looked it up on the Internet and found out that it's a secret society that isn't so secret because anyone can look it up on the Internet. *Lame.*

Anyway, we've decided to come up with a better name than "Skull and Bones," since skulls are kinds of bones and so that's like calling something "Pumpkin and Pie" or "Plant and Garden." It's just silly. I can't believe how many presidents have been in secret societies. *That we know of...*

We need a name that means something to us.

How about something like this?

Kind of creepy

Okay, then this:

~~SCS~~? School Celebrity Summit. Like this year is a mountain that we have to climb to gain school celebrity?

Weird.

Okay, here:

L and I

I like it

Initial Observations about

at Stephen Decatur Sr. Elementary

Gretchen Meyer

Has a blond streak in her hair. Looks like she might wear makeup, though it could just be cherry-flavored ChapStick.

Why doesn't Cherry ChapStick look like that on us?

Has an older sister who is the same age as Melody, and they don't get along *(Gretchen's sister and Melody) (and, really, who can blame her?) (Gretchen's sister)*

Gretchen's parents own the Jet ski rental shop on the lake.

Lisa Kovac

Lives only with her mom, who is really, really skinny

I need to eat a big sandwich!

Lisa has a cell phone that takes pictures and videos and has the Internet on it.

I drive a very shiny car!

She's always talking about different shampoos and skin-care products.

FEED ME!

JANE ASTLEY

Always gets the lead in the school plays, even though Lydia has a much better singing voice.

Injustice!

Her mom is just as giggly as she is, but her dad emails people on his PDA during every school event.

My mom thinks he's really rude.

So do Daddy and Papa Dad.

She can never just stand like a normal human being.

Sukie Thoms

What's in those pockets?
It's a mystery!

Very mysterious. Is often absent from class and gets picked up and dropped off by a mysterious black *No, dark green* a dark car. May or may not be in the federal witness protection program. MYSTERY. Other popular girls very protective of her. Quiet.

Quiet and full of mysterious Mystery.

On the field hockey team.

A mysterious game.

I don't know how it's played.

It's that mysterious.

Good Places to Make
OBSERVATIONS

1. Rehearsals for the school musical
   I'll be in charge of that

2. Sports teams — mostly field hockey because of Sukie *I have no idea how to play field hockey*
   I guess you're going to have to learn. *We'll see.*

3. The talent show
   We have to work up a routine for me.

4. The lake
   I'm not the greatest swimmer.

We've got our work cut out for us.

Experiment #1

Blond Streaking

We have observed (see Gretchen's Page) that Gretchen has a blond streak in her hair, so we're going to try to dye a blond streak in Lydia's hair.

Even though my hair is already blond

There's no way that Daddy or Papa Dad would let me dye my hair, and your Mom lets Melody dye hers black.

Mom doesn't let Melody do anything, Melody just does it.

We should ask her how.

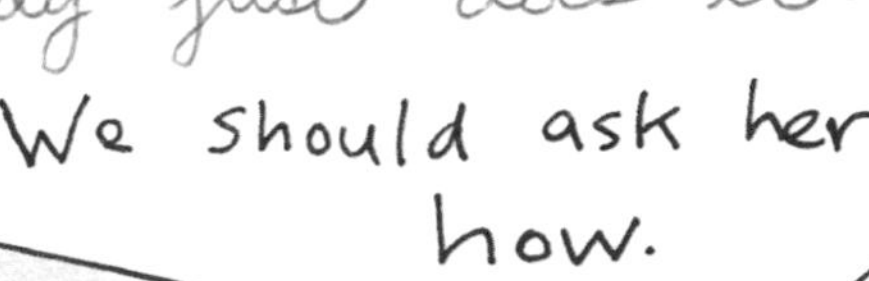

So we asked Melody how a person would go about dyeing their hair.

How would a person go about dyeing their hair?
Doo dee doo, just wondering.

We said it that way instead of saying "How would **WE** go about dyeing **OUR** hair?" So that she wouldn't be able to tell Lydia's mom about it because we really could have been talking about anyone. *Just making light conversation!*

Melody told us that if a person wanted to dye their hair a lighter color, a person would need some bleach.

Lydia, do you really want to try this?

Yes!!

But where are we going to get the hair dye?

Melody said that we don't need hair dye, we just need bleach.

Where are we going to get the bleach?

My mom has some under the kitchen sink.

I don't think that we're supposed to use that kind of bleach. I think we need a special bleach.

Don't be silly, we just have to use a lot of conditioner and my hair will be nice and soft.

You're going to smell like the janitor's Closet.

Saturday Night

In preparation for the DYEING EXPERIMENT, we have

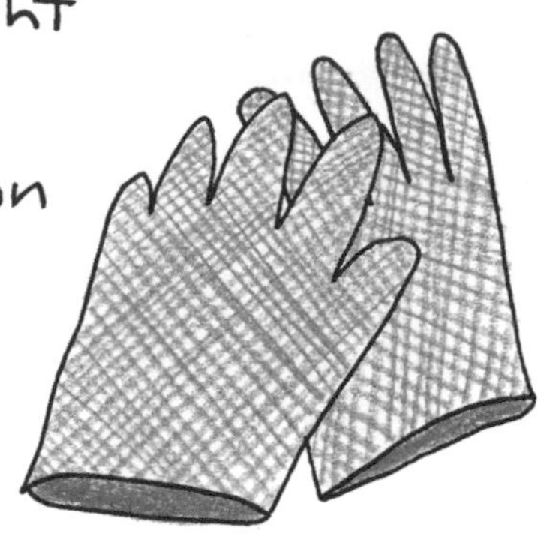

My mom's rubber cleaning gloves

and

bleach from the cabinet underneath our kitchen sink, and a basting brush that we'll use to apply the bleach to Lydia's (my) head.

And possible places on Lydia's head to bleach

Copying Gretchen

perfect!

Hey!!

We put the bleach right above Lydia's ear and used the instructions that we found on a box of hair dye that Lydia's mom had thrown out.

Almost immediately Lydia began to feel a burning sensation, so we knew it was working.

This feels bad.
Look, it's turning the Basting brush white.

As Lydia's mom says,

Sometimes you have to suffer for Beauty!

But I pointed out that she usually says that when she takes us out for ice cream and doesn't get any for herself, NOT when she feels like a small patch of her head is on fire.

10 minutes later.

Okay, that experiment wasn't a total success.

I'm bald!!! My hair fell out!!

You have an eensy-weensy bald patch.
The hair will grow back. Probably.

The skin is all red and bumpy and it hurts!!!

So while Lydia is running to her mom, I'll draw some ways we can cover up her really very small red bumpy bald patch.

Oh my gosh, Mrs. Goldblatt is SCREAMING.

LYDIA BEFORE NEW Haircut
Bald patch
Crying because Mrs. Goldblatt yelled at her for two hours. And because my head hurts!
LYDIA AFTER NEW HAIRCUT!
Hair layered to cover patch
Happy!
I think you've drawn me happier than I really am.
Aren't you happy we've learned something new?
Shut up.

Monday

Everyone is looking at my bald patch!!!

No one can see it. We did a good job of covering it up.

Lisa noticed, and she just haaaaaaaad to make a Comment.

What did she say?

"Nice haircut."

Maybe she just liked the way you're doing your hair now?

I don't think so.

OBSERVATION #2

SUKIE THOMS HAS A HOBBY

Did you see what Sukie was making on the bus this morning?

No, I was doing my math homework on the bus this morning.

Julie! You're supposed to be observing!!

So sorry that I'm not willing to fail math to ogle Sukie. What was she doing?

I think she was knitting a hat.

Maybe you could ask her to knit you a hat.

Why would I need a hat?

no reason.

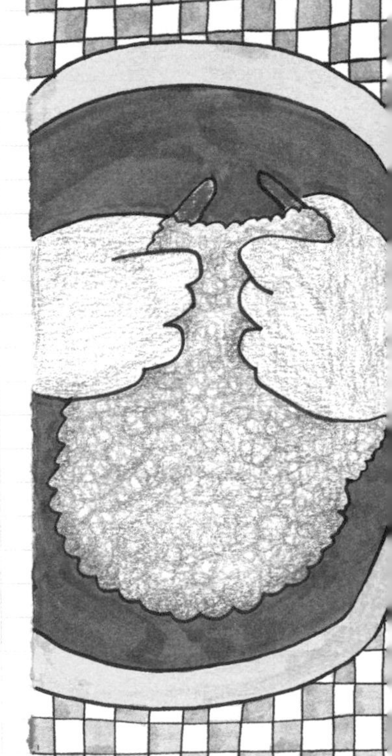

EXPERIMENT #2

Knit Wit

very clever

Because we have observed Sukie knitting, we have decided to learn how to Knit. Once we know how, it will be easier to approach Sukie for closer observation.

So, I see that you are knitting.
That is true, I am knitting.
You know, I knit everything that I am currently wearing.
Wow! You are very talented! Be my friend right now!

Because Lydia is still in hot water with her mom, we asked my dads if they could help us learn how to knit. Neither of them know how, but Papa Dad took us to the Yarn Store.

The lady at the yarn store was nice, but she kept making us touch all the different skeins of yarn.

Knitters call balls of yarn "skeins."

We are going to be such good knitters— we already know the language.

The Yarn Lady told us all about the different kinds of needles

We have metal, bamboo, plastic, circular...

Are there any battery-operated needles that can just knit a sweater for you?

Oh, aren't you cute. No.

And she showed us a book on

HOW TO KNIT

I'm a little confused.

I'm a lot confused.

Of course, Papa Dad made us take an oath before he bought us the supplies

Julie Graham-Chang and Lydia Goldblatt do solemnly swear that we will actually learn to knit and not just give up after two days like we did with the telescope and the aquarium and the electric keyboard.
We swear!
Swear on the knitting book.

October

We are going to be knitters!

We have knitting needles and yarn!

We're practically knitters already!!

Okay, according to the knitting book, the first thing that we have to do is "cast on," which means that we have to get the yarn on the needle.

Step 1: Make a slip knot

So far, knitting is totally easy.

We'll have the sweater that we promised to make Papa Dad done in no time!

Totally.

Step 2: Put slip knot on needle

Like this

step 3: Double cast-on

Hold string like this

Okay.

Then do this

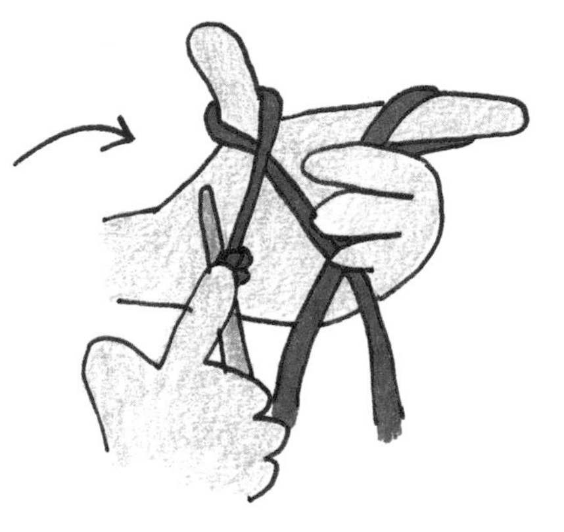

What?

Then this

You're kidding me.

Try it. You try it!

This is harder than it looks.

Maybe we could just make a braid out of the yarn.

How are we going to make a sweater out of a braid?

We tried for about an hour to do a double cast-on, after which we had something that looked like this

Which didn't really look like the picture in the book.

So we decided to take a break in order to clear our heads (and to get a snack), *and when we came back, we found this.*

It is going to take us forever to untangle this yarn.

Now I understand why Mr. Chang named your cat "Bad Cat."

True.

We managed to get the yarn off of Bad Cat (*she bit me!*) (she's <u>bad</u>!!) and we're going to hide the yarn stuff at Lydia's house (*so that Julie's cat can't eat it*) (and so Papa Dad won't see that we haven't been able to get the yarn onto the needles).

But we don't have the time to figure out how to knit right now because it's

SCHOOL MUSICAL AUDITION TIME!!

Papa Dad is going to kill me! *We'll work on knitting later!*

Every year Lydia auditions and hopes for a great lead role...

...and every year Jane Astley gets the lead role and Lydia gets a small part that was supposed to be played by a boy.

OBSERVATION #3

Last year Jane's audition song was from the musical Wicked. Lydia sang "Wouldn't It Be Loverly?" from My Fair Lady, which everyone has already heard a million, billion times.

I had the sheet music available!

But you've used it as an audition song every year for the past 3 years!!

It's a classic song!!!

So we figure that

Newer, More Exciting Song + Lydia's Awesome Singing Voice =

BETTER ROLE!

I'd like to thank the Academy...

To find a new song for Lydia, we polled (that means "asked") different people for creative song suggestions.

Lydia's Mom
How about "All That Jazz" from Chicago? You can do jazz hands and it will be soooo cute!!

Melody
Queen's "Bohemian Rhapsody." Sing the whole thing. Everyone will love it. Don't do jazz hands.

Daddy
How about "Defying Gravity" from Wicked? I have the original cast recording if you want to hear it.

"Don't stop Believing," by Journey! No, "I will Survive," by Gloria Gaynor! No, no, wait, "In-A-Gadda-Da-Vida," by Iron Butterfly!

We've gone over the songs. Melody's song is nearly 7 minutes long, and it doesn't make any sense. Melody is so weird.

I liked Lydia's mom's suggestion, but then we remembered that it was her mom who suggested "Wouldn't It Be Loverly?" three years ago. And I guess we know how well that turned out.

Daddy's song was perfect. So perfect that Jane sang it last year.

UNFAIR.

We've decided to ignore Mr. Graham's suggestions because he and Mr. Chang were laughing a lot when he was coming up with ideas. We don't think that they are entirely trustworthy.

It's like the time that Papa Dad offered us chopped liver. He was giggling then, too.

IT WAS GROSS.

Then Papa Dad suggested the Mattress Kingdom theme song because we're always singing it around the house.

We are no longer listening to Mr. Graham. Agreed. But we still have to knit him a sweater.

I've decided to sing "On My Own" from Les Miserables. It's a musical about being miserable during the French Revolution. It's a very adult song.

OBSERVATION #3 ½

(Still relating to Jane's audition last year)

Jane always looks really, really girly, which is probably why she gets the female roles.

What we need to do is make absolutely certain that Steve, the director, understands that I am a girl who should be given a girl role. Right!

THINGS THAT MAKE GIRLS GIRLY

They're a girl's best friend!

I thought I was your best friend.

It's a line from a song!

LYDIA'S TRANSFORMATION!

One whole week later...

So we really thought that Lydia would be the obvious choice for the role of Maria (the lead female role for The Sound of Music). The outfit, the song—

That Stupid Song!!!

It's a really well-liked song. Apparently.

FOUR OTHER GIRLS SANG THE SAME SONG.

And then, it happened. It was awful.

I panicked, and I could only remember one song that wasn't the song that everyone else had already performed.

When you need Your Umm Yum Yummy Sleeeep...
When you want that Umm Yum Yummy Feeeee!
Come to the Kingdoooooom!! Mattress Kingdom! Umm Yummy Yum!
Steve the Director
Ms. Finch the Assistant Director

Steve the Director called my mom last night to tell her that I was dressed inappropriately for school!!!

Oh no!

And he said that my song choice was odd!

Well, we knew that was going to happen.

Your Papa Dad put that song in my head!! Then my mom told me that I'm not allowed to wear makeup until I'm 13! It's not like I wanted to wear makeup all the time, but I did want the <u>option</u> of wearing makeup.

What about for Halloween?

I don't know!

Good news! Lydia got a part in The Sound of Music!

It's not a lead.
She gets to be in the Nun chorus.
It's not even a speaking part.
At least you got a girl role.
Oh goody.
I'm going to be on the stage crew.

The good thing about Lydia being a nun *I'm not a nun, I'm just playing the role of a nun!* Fine, the good thing about Lydia playing the role of a nun is that she can closely observe Jane, who has the lead role, and Gretchen, who is playing the role of the Baroness.

OBSERVATION #4

ALL OF THE POPULAR GIRLS HAVE

Even though students aren't allowed to have cell phones at school, we've noticed that Sukie will have one right on her desk in front of Ms. Mulligan and she never seems to get in trouble for it.

We're going to ask our parents for cell phones, and we've come up with good arguments as to why we need them:

1. It is a great big world, and if we have cell phones, we will never be lost!

So true!

2. We will be able to use our cell phones to find out what the weather will be like (if our cell phones have Internet access)! *How convenient!*

3. We can use our cell phones as flashlights!

Despite our careful preparations, our well-rehearsed requests were denied.

Sweetie, maybe when you're older we can talk about it.

Until then, you'll just have to make do with maps. And looking out the window (if it's white, it's snowing!). And, if you're good, I'll show you how to use a light switch!

Oh goody.

That's the spirit!

And how exactly are you going to pay your cell phone bills?
But Mom...
Are you just going to prune the money tree in the backyard?
But Mom...
Because I already pruned it to pay for your haircut.
We have a money tree in our backyard?
Stay out of this, Melody.

Because simply asking for a cell phone didn't work (at all), we have come up with

Problem: our parents don't think that we need cell phones, so they won't let us have cell phones.

Solution: show them that we do need cell phones!

If our parents need to find us and they can't, they'll see how useful cell phones are!

So we're going to run away from home for a very, very, very short time.

We're not even running away— we're strolling away from home.

Shuffling away from home.

Wandering away from home.

If we're away from home just long enough for our parents to be worried, our parents will realize that we need cell phones for our own safety. True!

Now all we have to figure out is

Where to GO?

We could go to the library?

No, the librarians are always really nosy. We need to go somewhere where no one will call our parents.

The mall?

How would we get there?

~~Papa Dad could drive us~~

Maybe we should just go to someone's house.

Probably. But who?

Someone whose parents don't have our parents' phone numbers?

Right. This is going to require some thinking.

OPTION A

Michelle Jacks

Friendly and lives close to school.

But her mom is in my mom's Book Club.

Poop.

OPTION B

Bernice Wyatt

Lives near your bus stop.

She called me "Goldbladder" during gym because she was trying to impress Lisa Kovac. Also, she often smells like a ham sandwich.

OPTION C

Gretchen Meyer

Yeah right.

It would be a really good way to Observe her.

Next!

OPTION D

Roland Asbjørnsen

New kid in school.

Speaks with a funny accent.

Very friendly.

Lives near the school.

This could work!

December

Were you just talking with Roland?

Yeah, I asked him for help with the math work.

But you're good at math.

It was an excuse to talk to him!

Oh! Duh. What did he say?

It was kind of hard to understand him, but I think that we're invited to his house after school so he can help us with math.

But I don't need math help.

Julie! The Plan!!

Right!

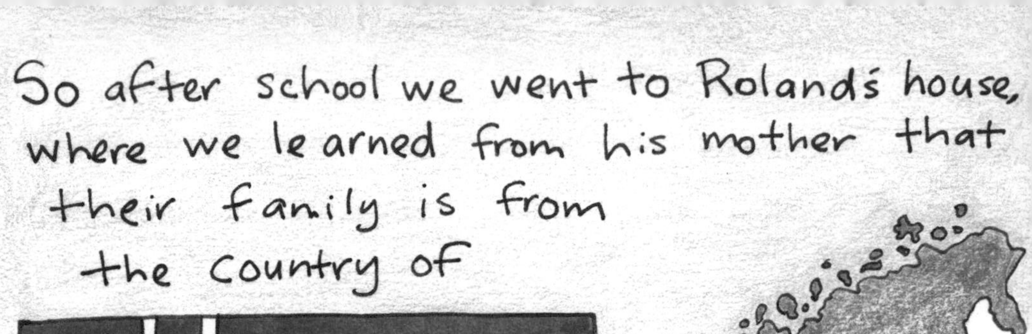
So after school we went to Roland's house, where we learned from his mother that their family is from the country of

NORWAY

norway looks a little like a giraffe with no legs

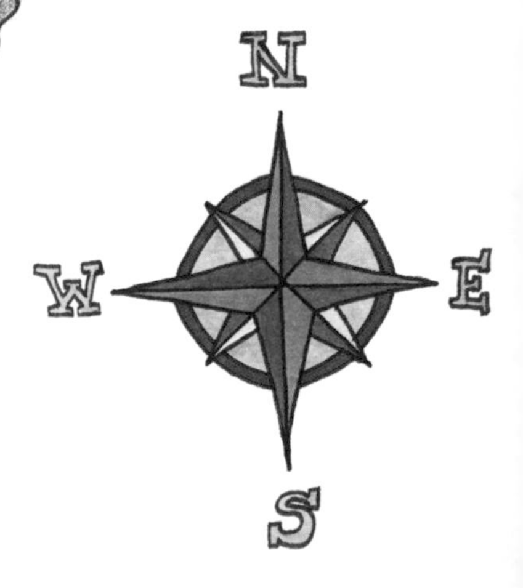
N
W
E
S

Mrs. Asbjørnsen was really excited that Roland has new friends and she hugged us. A lot.

There was so much hugging!

She was really strong.

No kidding.

We watched her squeeze something out of what looked like a tube of toothpaste onto a cracker and then she ate it!

The toothpaste smelled like a fish!!!

UNRELATED OBSERVATION
Mrs. Asbjørnsen really likes trolls.
She collects them.
Lots of them.
Roland's house is full of them.
They're staring at us!
Aaaaaaaahhhh!!!

Things seemed to be going well. Roland's mom didn't make us eat the stinky fish paste and we actually ended up helping Roland with some of the more advanced math problems.

We were pretty sure of how our parents would react when we finally came home.

You're alive! We were worried!

Oh, if only we could have had a way to call you!

You two must have cell phones so that this will never, ever happen again!

It didn't actually happen like that.

The experiment wasn't a total failure — now we know that we have to stay out later than 4:30 in the afternoon.

Right.

LEARN IMPROVE

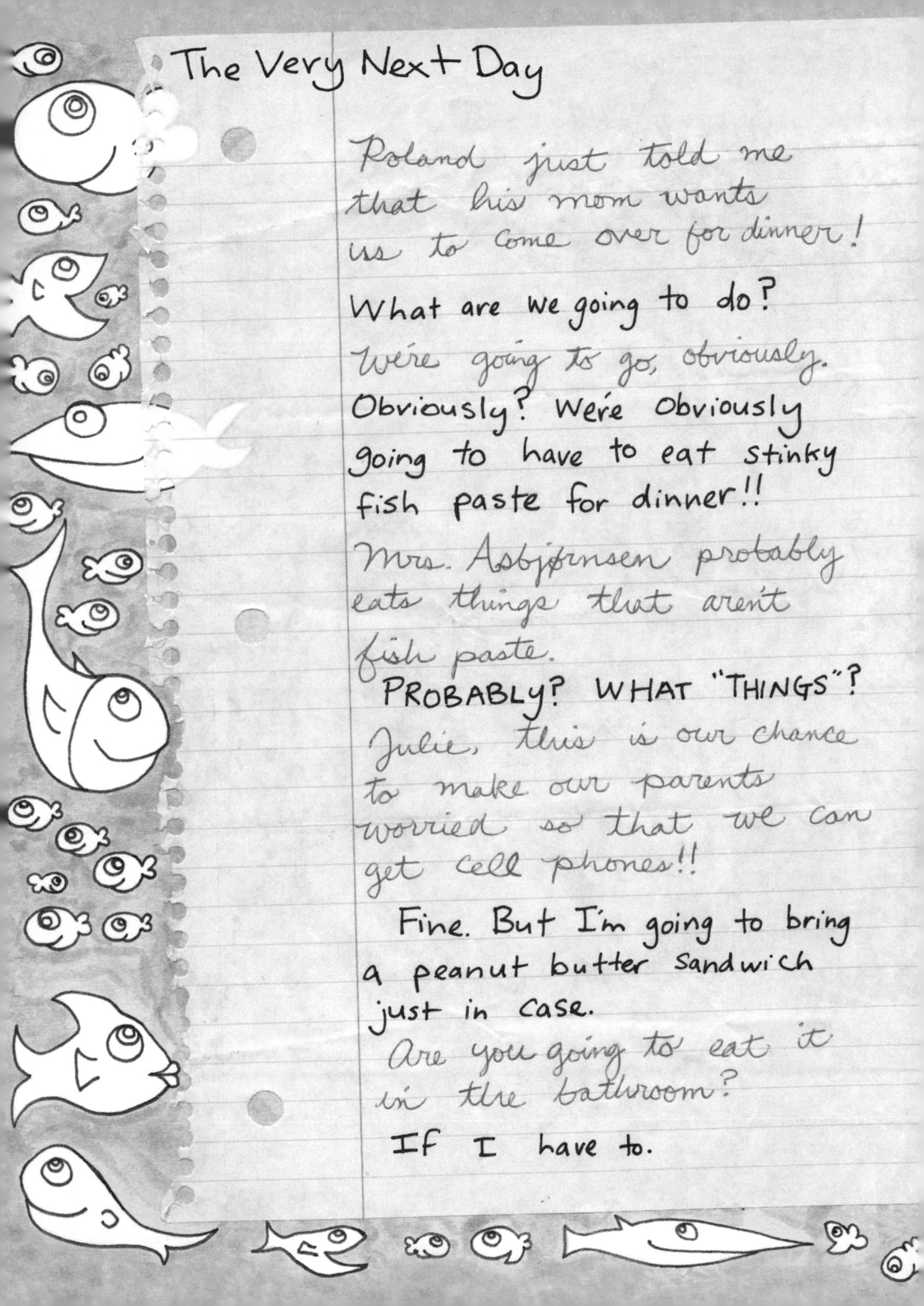

The Very Next Day

Roland just told me that his mom wants us to come over for dinner!

What are we going to do?

We're going to go, obviously.

Obviously? We're Obviously going to have to eat stinky fish paste for dinner!!

Mrs. Asbjørnsen probably eats things that aren't fish paste.

PROBABLY? WHAT "THINGS"?

Julie, this is our chance to make our parents worried so that we can get cell phones!!

Fine. But I'm going to bring a peanut butter sandwich just in case.

Are you going to eat it in the bathroom?

If I have to.

The PLAN

PART 2

1. We go to Roland's house for dinner.

Problem: how do we get home? It will be too dark to walk and my parents will **FREAK OUT.**

2. We tell the Asbjørnsens that your parents' cars are broken and then they drive us home.

Both of them at the same time?

We can tell them that Papa Dad backed into Daddy's car with his car.

That's a lot of lying.

Trust me, it will work!

3. We bring peanut butter sandwiches in case Roland's mom makes us eat something weird.

THINGS WE LEARNED AT our Dinner with the ASBJØRNSENS

1. Roland has two older brothers

Peder

Senior in high school. Wants to be called "Pete" but the family still calls him "Peder."

Totally cute.

Anders

Thirteen. Knows Melody! He says that she's "pretty and nice," therefore he is Completely insane.

Roland's father is named

Dinner was actually pretty good

We had hamburgers!

Mrs. Åsbjørnsen said that they are called "Karbonader."

Whatever, you didn't have to eat a soggy peanut butter sandwich while sitting on a toilet.

I was pretty happy about that.

The dessert was super yummy.

I didn't have any.

It was called "Jordbærrullekake".

I call it "Strawberry Death Cake of Death."

Sorry you couldn't have any.

Despite the Jordbaerrullekake (Norwegian words are crazy!) we had a really nice time at the Asbjørnsens'.

Mrs. Asbjørnsen even offered to give us a ride home, so we didn't have to lie about Daddy and Papa Dad's cars!

So at around eight at night, she drove us home. She went to my house first.

And that's when things got **BAD**.

First came the hugs. The hugs were good.

They were really worried and I started to feel bad.

But we thought our plan was working.

And then came **THE ANGER.**

DO YOU KNOW HOW WORRIED WE HAVE BEEN? DO YOU HAVE ANY IDEA?

WHEN I CALLED THE GRAHAM-CHANGS AND FOUND OUT THAT YOU WEREN'T THERE, I ALMOST DIED.
I am so very apologies! I sot you knew where de girls were! I am feeling very terrible!
I am so disappointed in you.
It was awful.

Then Mrs. Goldblatt took Lydia home. Daddy and Papa Dad made me go to my room while they had a long talk with Mrs. Asbjørnsen.

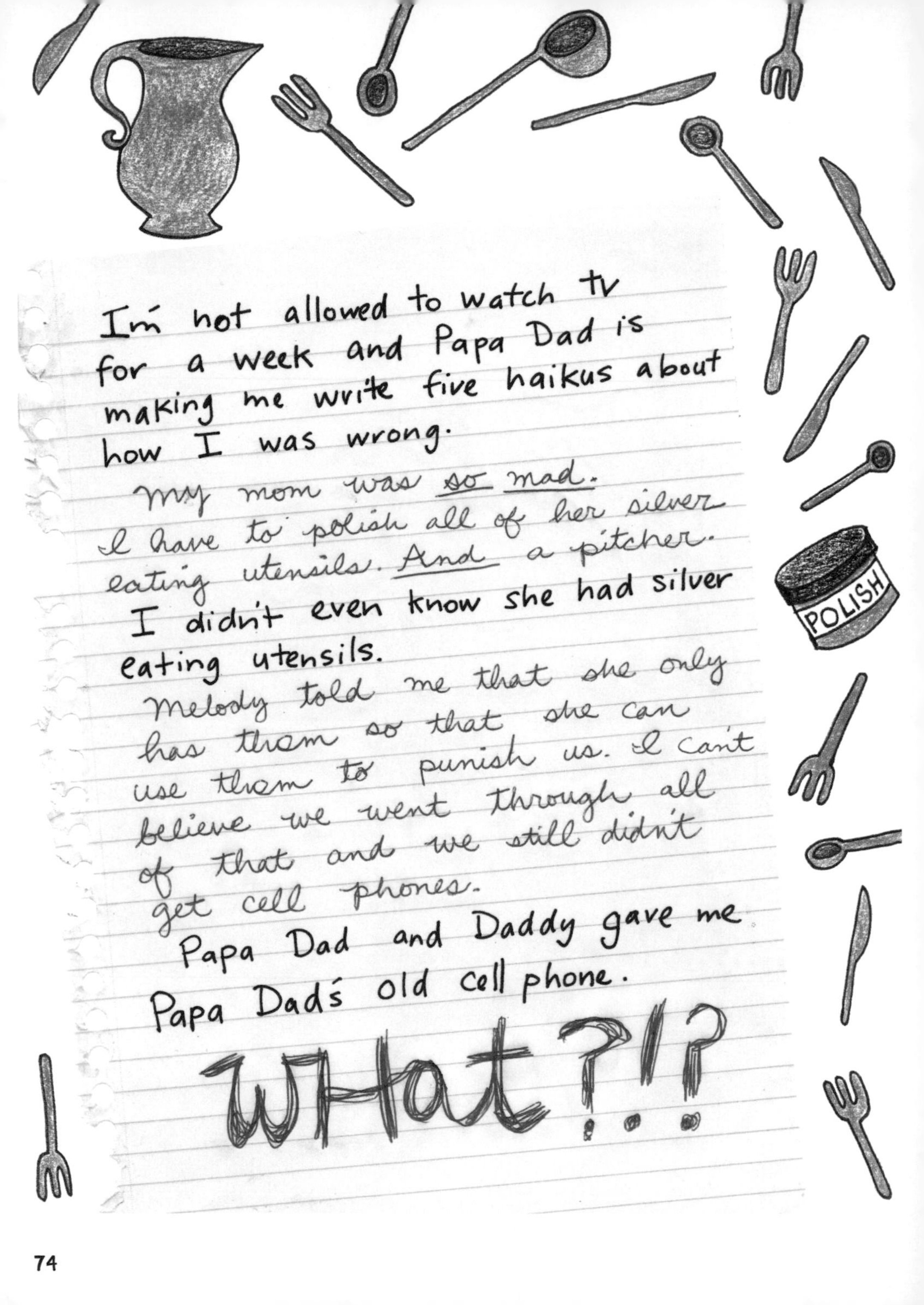
I'm not allowed to watch tv
for a week and Papa Dad is
making me write five haikus about
how I was wrong.
My mom was so mad.
I have to polish all of her silver
eating utensils. And a pitcher.
I didn't even know she had silver
eating utensils.
Melody told me that she only
has them so that she can
use them to punish us. I can't
believe we went through all
of that and we still didn't
get cell phones.
Papa Dad and Daddy gave me
Papa Dad's old cell phone.
WHat?!?
POLISH

JULIE'S NEW
(Papa Dad's really, really old)
CELL PHONE

Screen doesn't work, so I don't know who is calling me and I can't call anyone unless I have their phone numbers memorized

Antenna all chewed up by Bad Cat

phone kept together with duct tape

numbers on the buttons have been rubbed off

Aren't you just soooooooo jealous of my super awesome cell phone?

Okay, not so much.

MY 5 SORRY HAIKUS

A haiku is a Japanese type of poetry. It's three lines long (which is good when you have to write FIVE of them). The first line has to be 5 syllables, the second has to be 7 syllables, and the third is like the first.

I didn't come home
I went to the Asbjørnsens'
Their dad's name is Thor.

I should have told you
That I was with Norwegians
Alas! I did not.

Daddy was worried
And so was poor Papa Dad
They were so upset.

I was really wrong
Quite totally extra wrong
Really very wrong.

I am so sorry
So sorry sorry sorry
A lot of sorry.

So our maybe-not-so-well-thought-out plan didn't work out so well.

I didn't get a cell phone at all, and Julie's isn't cool AT ALL.

It's got a certain vintage charm. No, it doesn't

But we have learned that EXPERIMENTS THAT MAKE OUR PARENTS WORRIED ARE

VERY, VERY BAD

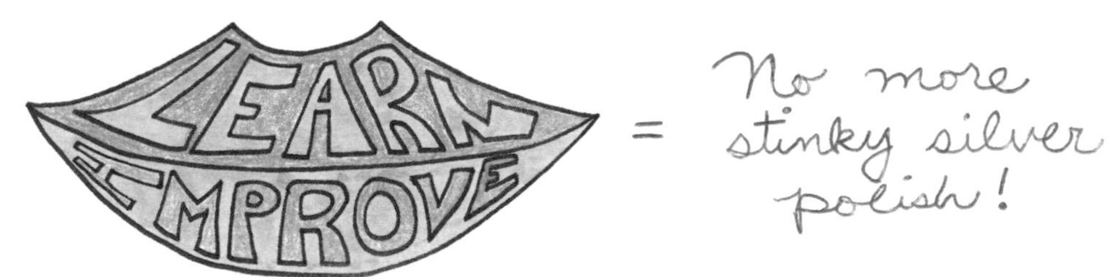

= No more stinky silver polish!

So we're going to refocus our energies on Observing during musical rehearsals.

After the winter holidays.

January

SOME OBSERVATIONS

1. Jane's mom comes to rehearsal a lot and likes to make helpful suggestions to Steve the Director.

2. Steve the Director seems to be kind of annoyed by Jane's mom.
3. So does Jane.

ANOTHER (probably more useful) OBSERVATION

Gretchen and Jane talk about boys. **ALL THE TIME.**

We usually can't hear what they're saying. But you know they're talking about boys when they start to whisper.

We've heard them say a couple of different names, but we're not sure if Gretchen and Jane like or hate the boys.

We MUST Learn More!

If they like boys that we don't like, do we have to like them? I don't know. Maybe?

The BOYS

BOY #1 — Michael Cavelleri

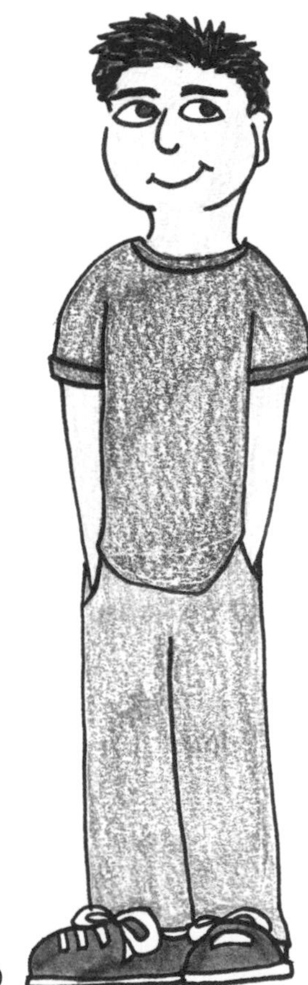

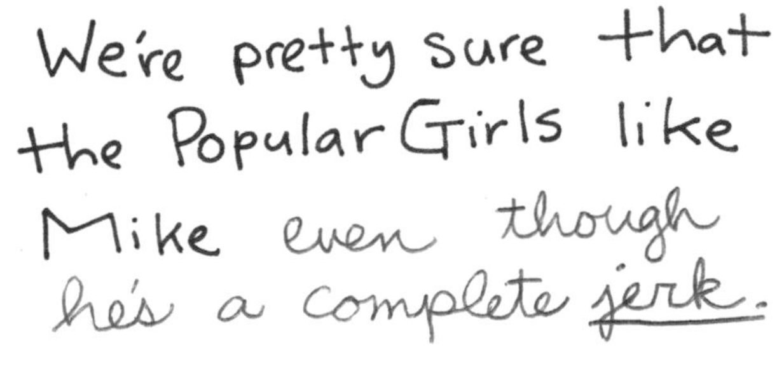

We're pretty sure that the Popular Girls like Mike *even though he's a complete jerk.*

He's the one who first started calling Lydia "Goldbladder" in 3rd grade.

I HATE HIM.

It's going to be really hard at this point to see his good side.

BOY #2

Ross Denenberg

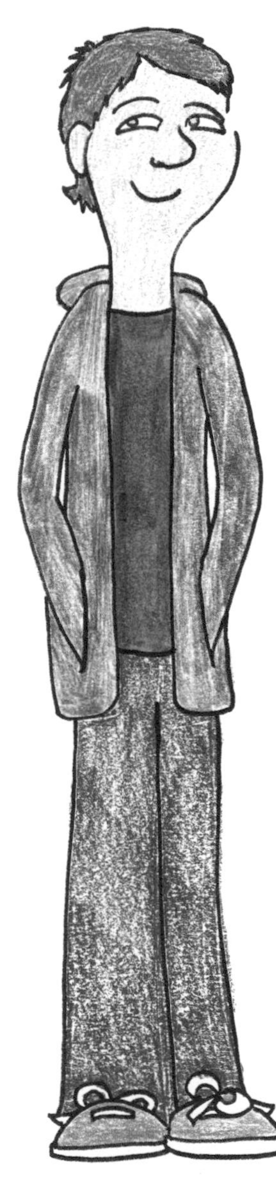

Friends with Mike Cavelleri, but has never called Lydia "Goldbladder."

He's very nice.

He's supertall, and Ms. Mulligan is always asking him to get books from on top of the high shelves.

I could like him if I had to, even though he hangs out with Mike.

I could too. If I had to.

So that's a relief.

Boy #3

Jamie Burke

We don't think that the Popular Girls like Jamie very much.

He's a complete spaz.

He shoved 14 powdered-sugar mini-doughnuts into his mouth yesterday.

Maybe if we talk loudly about how lame he is, we can start a conversation with Gretchen.

Wouldn't that be mean?

I don't think that Jamie cares what anyone thinks about him.

BOY/MAN #4

Mr. Peters

The other 5th grade teacher. The Popular Girls talk about him **ALL THE TIME.**

He wears jeans while he's teaching at least once a week.

Michelle Jacks is in his class and she says he's really nice.

He has a very small beard right under his lower lip, which is totally cool.

It is? I guess so.

Are you nervous about

OPENING NIGHT?

Not really.

But all those people will be watching you.

No, all those people will be watching Jane. I'm just a Background Nun.

But what if you mess up?

Are you _trying_ to make me nervous?

No, no, I'm just being nervous for you. So you don't have to be.

Umm... Thank you?

You're welcome! Break a leg!

OPENING NIGHT!

Jane has actually broken her leg in a freak rodeo accident!

I was attacked by an escaped rodeo bull!
Freakish!

I'll say!

And as Lydia had memorized all of Jane's lines, songs, and dances, she had to step into the lead role!

Help us, Lydia! You're our only hope!
Start the show. I'm ready.
Bless you, Lydia Goldblatt!

Everyone was tremendously nervous that she would mess up, but her performance was flawless in every way!

Gretchen and the other Popular Girls were very grateful and impressed, but not as impressed as

The BROADWAY PRODUCERS in the AUDIENCE!

And then a unicorn came by!
And barfed up pirate treasure!!
And as soon as we clean off the gold, we'll be both rich and famous!
Eww... but thanks.
Sorry. And you're welcome.
Okay, here's what really happened...

OPENING NIGHT!

Lydia acted like a nun and sang very well.

Jane's mother was super happy with her performance.

Aaaand Mr. Peters was in the audience...

With his GIRLFRIEND!

I was backstage, so I didn't see her.

Me neither. Gretchen and Jane recognized her from the time that they saw her down at the lake with him. They said that she isn't a natural redhead and that she has a tattoo and her dress was ugly. I wish that my wimple hadn't kept falling over my eyes. Then I could have seen better and I would know better what kind of dresses not to wear.

She wore a dress to the lake?

No, she wore a dress to the show!! I wonder if we could look her up on the Internet. Would your dads let us use their computer?

Maybe.

DADDY AND PAPA DAD's RULES for the INTERNET

1. NO INTERNET WITHOUT PERMISSION.

2. NO INTERNET UNLESS THERE IS A PARENT PRESENT IN THE ROOM.

3. THE PARENT IN THE ROOM RESERVES THE RIGHT TO TURN THE COMPUTER OFF AT ANY TIME.

4. THE PARENT IN THE ROOM RESERVES THE RIGHT TO MAKE COMMENTS ABOUT WHATEVER WE'RE LOOKING AT.

Maybe we should go to the library

Yeah.

Going to the library to use the Internet can really be a pain in the butt.

First, there's always Creepy Guy who plays Computer Solitaire All The Time.
And what are we working on?
nuthin'.
And then there's Cheerful Librarian who is always up in everybody's business.

But we managed to get online, and then we started our Search—

LYDIA GOLDBLATT, INTERNET SLEUTH

OUR INTERNET SEARCH

First, we typed in

MR. PETERS'S GIRLFRIEND

Which led to a bunch of articles with the words "Mr.," "Peters's," and "girlfriend" in them. ~~Boo.~~ Then we typed

"MR. PETERS'S GIRLFRIEND"

Because you have to put things in quotes.

Well, now we know. And that search resulted in NOTHING.

So we'd probably need Mr. Peters's first name.

Or his girlfriend's whole entire name. Let's search for pictures of puppies instead.

You give up too easily!

The library printer is not my friend.

BRILLIANT IDEAS FOR FINDING OUT MR. PETERS'S FIRST NAME OR HIS GIRLFRIEND'S WHOLE ENTIRE NAME

1. Ask him?

How am I supposed to do that?

So, anyway, what's your first name? And your girlfriend's whole entire name? Oh, and could you spell that for me?
How would you like my cell phone number as well?
This is unrealistically easy!

2. Go to the lake and hope she shows up?

Nobody goes to the lake in the middle of February.

Are you ladies done now? I'd join you but I HAVE NO SWEATER TO KEEP ME WARM.

I hope it will be warmer at Buck's Valley next month. Me too.

BUCK'S VALLEY

Every year the 5th grade class goes to Buck's Valley for a week to sleep in cabins and learn about nature.

Melody hated it when she went and almost came home early. Mom told me that she didn't like her cabinmates.

Do you think that we'll get to be in a cabin together?

Maybe we'll be in a cabin with Gretchen! We'll see when we get our room assignments.

You will not believe what my mom bought me for the trip to BUCK's Valley!!!

A CELL PHONE FOR CHILDREN!

It's horrible! It looks like I'm talking into a big plastic bug! I might as well come to school wearing diapers! The buttons are the size of dimes!!! I can't be seen with this!

Maybe you could paint it black? Or dark blue, so it looks like a scarab. Aren't scarabs cool?

Maybe if you're an Ancient Egyptian!!

I'm just trying to help. At least you know who you're calling.

I don't know why you're complaining. I'm the only person you'd call, anyway.

March

We are packed and ready to go to

Buck's Valley!

We have made certain to pack

1. Scented Lotion: we don't want to be known as the dry, stinky girls.

2. Pens, colored pencils, markers, and glue, because we need to Observe and Record!

3. An extra pillowcase where we can hide The Handbook.

4. Melody said to bring extra socks and underwear and to hide them.

You can't trust anything that Melody says.

She's so weird.

OUR BUNK ASSIGNMENTS

You are so, so lucky, I almost hate you

JULIE'S BUNK	LYDIA'S BUNK
Gretchen Meyer Lucky Lisa Kovac Also lucky Bernice Wyatt Maybe not so lucky	Deirdre Nutter, Captain of the Field Hockey Team Maxine Harrington, also on the Field Hockey Team Eve Eaton Also on the Field Hockey Team!!!

You get to observe and mingle! All I can do is listen to conversations about boring Field Hockey!

Isn't Sukie on the Field Hockey team?

She's not in my bunk, so who cares?

Roland is stuck in a bunk with Jamie Burke.

BUCK'S VALLEY

Julie's Bunk

trail to the lake

15

Teachers' Quarters + Bathrooms

17

19

14

16

21

20

18

13

Dining Hall

Campfire area

12

11

Lydia's Bunk

administrative offices

9

10

Infirmary + Bathrooms

8

Ropes Course area

3

7

1

6

4

2

5

There are two bunk beds in each cabin. Gretchen is on the top bunk over Lisa. (Lisa insisted on having the bottom bunk because she is afraid of heights, which seems ridiculous. Does she have a panic attack every time she climbs the stairs?) I'm on the other top bunk, which is cool because I've always wanted to have a bunk bed. Bernice is under me and keeps talking to Gretchen and Lisa about how much fun they're going to have. *She is so annoying.*

Our dining-room seating is assigned! Lame!

And we're still not at the same table!

I get to be at a table with Sukie and Lisa.

I get to be at a table with Roland and Michelle, so that's okay.

Ms. Mulligan is at my table.

It's weird to see her dressed in jeans and hiking boots.

I know! It's weird to see her eating.

What?

Do I have something on my face?

A NOTE UNFORTUNATELY WRITTEN DURING THE ROPES COURSE LECTURE ON SAFETY

Bernice snored ALL NIGHT.

All night? Were you awake the whole time?

A lot of the time. I'm so tired.

I'm pretty tired too. The Field Hockey Girls were playing mancala until one in the morning! That's what they're always doing when they're sitting together at lunch. They're really competitive.

Lisa and Gretchen were whispering a lot of stuff to each other.

Could you hear them? What were they saying?

Mostly they were complaining about Bernice's snoring.

Did you join in? Being annoyed with Bernice's snoring is something that you have in common with them!

I was just trying really hard to sleep.

So the idea was that as part of the Team Building part of the Ropes Course, we all had to help one another to climb a wall. It seemed really high up, but I decided not to be scared because I figured it was about as high up as a bunk bed. Maybe a little higher.

And now I'm in the infirmary.

Daddy is on his way to pick me up.

This sucks!

I'm going to miss out on the all-day hike and the marshmallow roasting and everything and my ankle is going to be taped up for a MONTH!

I will eat extra marshmallows just for you.

EVERYTHING IS HORRIBLE AND BAD!

I'm going to observe Everything and write everything down, I promise, so it will be like you were here the whole time, okay? And now you won't have to listen to Bernice snore, so that's good, right?

I guess.

Dear Julie,

After Daddy came and picked you up everyone was asking me what happened and how you were doing. Mike Cavelleri started telling people that you were attacked by a bear

But Gretchen told the truth and said that if Mike had been more helpful you probably wouldn't have fallen. I don't understand why she scolds him if she wants him to like her. ~~the~~ I must investigate this weird behavior.

Today we went on the All-Day walk, and all the boys kept trying to see who could climb the highest tree. Roland was about to climb when Outdoor Educator Bill got mad and told us that he didn't want to have to send anyone else home for broken bones.

come down.
I love your accent!
Okay!

Roland seemed relieved that he didn't have to climb, and Jane told him that she thought he would have done great. She was being all flirty! With Roland!!!?!

We worked on Survival Skills today. I was put in a group with Sukie, Ross, and Maxine, who is pretty funny. We were supposed to build a fire. Ross tried to take over, which annoyed Sukie and Maxine. I always thought that Sukie was quiet, but being around the other Field Hockey girls makes her a little scary. Ross backed off a little and they got the fire started. I collected the kindling.

At night we all sat around the campfire and roasted marshmallows. Jamie Burke burnt all of his and then burnt his mouth eating them. I don't think that Outdoor Educator Bill is going to miss Jamie.

stop that!

Lydia is back! I'm back!!!

THINGS LYDIA LEARNED at BUCK'S VALLEY

1. The Popular Girls (at least Gretchen, Lisa, and Jane) totally like Mike Cavelleri. But I thought Jane likes Roland? I think that Jane just flirts with everyone. It's what my mom calls "casting a wide net."

I don't get it. Neither do I. But Gretchen, Lisa, and Jane took tons and tons of pictures of Mike, so I guess they like him.

2. We definitely have to find boys to like.

3. I now know how to build a fire. Sort of.

The Problem with BOYS

We cannot Like Mike Cavelleri.

Impossible. It will never happen.

I would rather eat a bucket of chopped liver than like Mike Cavelleri.

I would rather bleach my whole head than like Mike Cavelleri.

I wouldn't have fallen off the wall if he hadn't been all snappy and pushy.

And he thinks he's so funny when he calls me "Goldbladder."

Why do they like him?

He's probably never mocked them or sprained their ankles. But it's better not to like him anyway, because at Buck's Valley Bernice seemed to like him and I overheard the Popular Girls laughing about it.

So who are you going to like?

Chuck Cavelleri

(brand-new object of Lydia's affections)

Chuck is Mike's older brother. He's in middle school already, so I'll get a head start on liking him.

THINGS WE KNOW ABOUT HIM

1. He wears many black tee shirts with bands on them, so we know which bands he likes.

2. While we were on the All-Day hike, Bill took a stick away from Mike, who told Ross that Chuck had taught him how to stick-fight because Chuck takes lessons.

3. He has never once called Lydia "Goldbladder."

Or talked to me.

Another PLAN

I'm going to convince my mom to let me take stick-fighting classes! Imagine how cool it will look if I have an older boyfriend!

Are you going to kiss him? If he's your boyfriend, you have to kiss him.

Who are you going to have a crush on?

I don't know. Nobody?

You could have a crush on Roland. He's nice.

I guess so. But I'm not going to kiss him.

What did your mom say about the stick-fighting lessons?

I called them "self-defense" lessons and she freaked out and demanded to know who was bullying me and gave me a speech about how violence is not the answer.

Oh no!

It's okay. I told her that I was just interested in stick-fighting because other kids were taking lessons and it sounded fun, and then she said I could go.

Wow. Are you scared that you're going to get hurt?

I hadn't thought about it.

Maybe you shouldn't.

And a week later

LYDIA'S FIRST DAY of ESKRIMA!

(stick-fighting)

Guru Taralanna

Okay, newbies, before you learn how to do sumbrada, contrada, sinawali, hubudubud, or sequidas, you're going to do some basic warm-ups!

50 jumping jacks! Starting now!

It was nice of Guru Taralanna to let me watch the lesson, although I'm pretty sure that if it weren't for my sprained ankle she would have made me participate.

It's sprained.
I believe you.
For now.

Chuck looked surprised to see Lydia, but all the other students looked surprised to see Lydia.

Maybe because Lydia was the only girl there.

The first day of class was not at all like I thought it would be.

I'm starting to wonder if stick-fighting is cool. None of the guys in the class were even slightly like the Popular Girls. What if I'm headed in the wrong direction?

Chuck seemed nice.
He hardly talked to me!!!

But he didn't hit you with a stick. That's promising, right?

I'm thinking of asking my mom if I can quit the stick-fighting lessons.
I THINK I JUST TOLD ROLAND THAT I HAD A CRUSH ON HIM IN MUSIC CLASS!
YOU DID WHAT??
He was helping to carry my stuff and I told him he was really nice, which was why I chose him to be the guy that I like, but now I think he thinks I really like him!!!
I don't think that boys are supposed to know about the crushes that we're supposed to have on them!
I don't think so either! Is he looking at me?
Yes.
What are we going to do?
Stupid fat love baby

Oh no no no no oh no
oh no oh no!!! Look
what Roland just gave to me
oh no no no no NO!!!!!!

Ode to Julie
by Roland Asbjørnsen

You like me and I like you
Which is great, because the feeling is mutual
And now we are very happy
in our mutual assurances.

I will never feed you strawberries
Because they might hurt you
And that would make me sad
which would be bad.

But you are very pretty and nice
And you draw very well
And I like the way you smell.

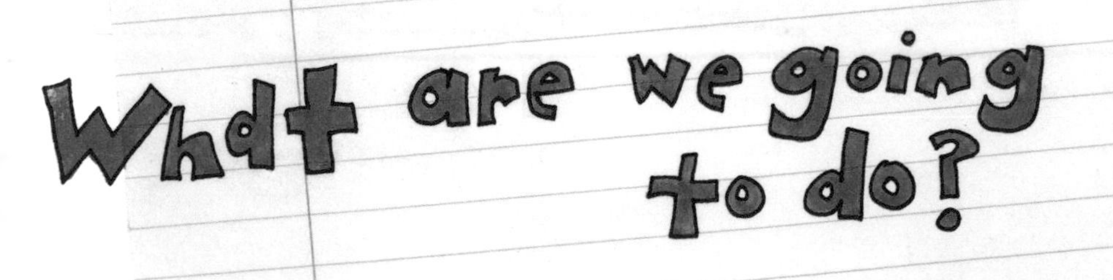

IDEAS to get ROLAND to NOT LIKE JULIE

1. Throw something at him, like a shoe or a textbook. **Problem:** Might get into trouble or lose a shoe.

2. Find out something to say that would deeply offend Norwegians and say it. "Your Karbonader is smelly and inedible!" "Trolls are weird and off-putting!" We may have to do some more research into that.

3. Tell him to stop liking me! *If I told you to stop liking ice cream, would you just stop?* I AM NOT ICE CREAM!

The Next Day

THE WORST THING THAT COULD HAPPEN EVER IN THE WORLD EVER

Roland showed his poem about Julie to Miss Blanche, the music teacher, who loved it.

Who shows their personal projects to teachers? We haven't shown this book to Ms. Mulligan. We haven't said, "Hey, Ms. Mulligan, why don't you have a look at all of our most personal thoughts?"

And now Miss Blanche wants to turn his poem into a song!

This is the most embarrassing thing in the world ever. I'm going to ask Daddy and Papa Dad to home-school me.

This will be perfect for the Spring Concert!

April

So we've talked it over, and we've come to the conclusion that

NOTHING IS WORKING.

We've tried to dress differently, we've tried to do our hair differently, we've tried to be brave while climbing a really high wall, and for what? Lydia's hair fell out and she has to keep taking stick-fighting classes and the whole elementary school chorus is going to be singing a song about how Roland Asbjørnsen thinks I smell nice!!

At least the song will be performed in Norwegian. No one will know it's about you.

Whatever.

Du liker meg og jeg liker deg...

But we can't give up. If we give up, we might as well just walk into middle school and ask everyone to make horrible fun of us.

So we have to do something. Something really big. Something bigger than bleach and pink clothing and sort-of-secret crushes on boys that we may or may not actually like. We need—

THE SCHOOL TALENT SHOW!

Oh no. Not again...

So here we are, once again, trying to decide on a song for Lydia to sing at the Talent Show. Last year Jamie Burke stole the show by doing a magic routine.

Pick a card, any card! Is it the nine of clubs?
I haven't picked a card yet.
You don't have to! I already magically know what you are going to pick! TA DA!!

Everyone thinks that Jamie is funny, but no one thinks he's cool. I want people to think that ~~I'm~~ we're cool. But Papa Dad overheard us discussing our plans, and he had an interesting sort of idea.

If you want for people to stop calling you "Goldbladder," you have to make people see that it doesn't bother you. You have to own it. There were a lot of words that people have used to be mean to me, but I knew they were stupid and I turned it around by embracing those words. Then instead of throwing word rocks at me it was like the mean people were throwing word cotton candy. It didn't matter.

Then Papa Dad found an old record and played it for us, which gave us an idea.

So we took the song that Papa Dad suggested, "Goldfinger," and changed the lyrics.

Goldbladder
She's the girl
The girl with the golden name
It brings her fame!

Such a Bold Matter
To have such a name
Nobody can be the same
She rocks this game!

Golden notes she will pour in your ear
But her name is what she holds so dear!
For this golden girl knows how to rock
Even though her name might shock

It's Goldbladder
Everytime
She takes the stage and starts to rhyme
It sounds sublime!

It's Goldbladder time!
A rocking good time!
This song is just fine!
GOldbladder time!

So much better than Roland's song, if we do say so ourselves.

One Week Later

I was in Eskrima class, and Chuck said, "Are you going to the talent show tomorrow night?"

Are you going to the talent show tomorrow night?

It wasn't like that at all! I told him, "Yes, are you?"

Yes, are you?

That definitely didn't happen. He said he was going.

He's totally in love with you.

Maybe I like stick-fighting.

I'm getting really nervous about tonight's performance.

I know! I'm really nervous for you.

AAAAAAAGGEHHHHH!!! You need to not be nervous, you need to be encouraging!

Sorry, sorry. You've got a great voice and you're going to do great, and like Papa Dad said, if you're brave and you act like you can take a joke then everyone will see that you're great.

Do you mean that?

Of course. If it were me, though, I'd be barfing. I'd barf until I barfed out all of my internal organs.

Now I'm more grossed-out than I am nervous.

See, I helped! I'm helpful.

Yes, you're incredibly helpful.

The talent show started off with Jane singing a song *as usual.*

Cleaned a lot of plates in Memphis, pumped a lot of pain down in New Orleans...

Some kids in Lydia's class did a stick-fighting demo.
I'm not that good yet.

Jamie started to do an act that seemed to involve singing and/or eating peanut butter, but Miss Blanche made him stop.

Oh sweetie, your artistic vision confuses me. Time to go, okay?

Then it was Lydia's turn.

Did you teach her this song?
Sorry, can't take credit.
Did you teach her this song?
I may have shown her the album.
Shhh!

SHE DID IT!

I DID IT!!!

She really did it! I thought that Papa Dad was never going to stop laughing.

Everyone was laughing!

But in a good way! In a really good way!!!

Gretchen and Sukie and even Mike all told me how good I was! Mike called me "Goldy"!

That's good, right?

Now that we have momentum, we must build on it!

Explain?

Yet another

Seeing how I've impressed everyone in the school with my song, we're going to try out for the field hockey team!

The doctor says my ankle is better, so I guess I can try out.

If we're on the field hockey team, we'll get closer to Sukie and maybe find out why she's so mysterious. Also, I think that the field hockey girls are good to have on your side.

They're scary, and bad to not have on your side.

The Next Day...

We got in! We got on the team! Deirdre Nutter congratulated me and told me that you were on the team as well! They were really impressed by how fast you can run.

No one really gets horribly hurt in field hockey, right?

You're so fast you'll outrun anyone trying to hit you with a hockey stick.

PEOPLE GET HIT WITH HOCKEY STICKS?

Oh my gosh Julie, I'm kidding, just kidding. Mostly.

WORST NEWS EVER

(besides the news that Roland's poem is being made into a song to be performed at the Spring Concert.)

LYDIA'S MOM WON'T LET HER BE ON the FIELD HOCKEY TEAM.

We went home and told our parents that we'd made the team...
You didn't even tell us that you were trying out.
This is great! I've always wanted an athlete in the family!
I fenced in college.
Yeah, but like a real athlete.
I'm ignoring that. Good for you, Sweetie!

But at Lydia's house...

Oh no. You are not joining the field hockey team. Not until you're finished with your Eskrima lessons.

But Mom...

But nothing. You begged for those lessons and you're not going to give them up to do another weird sport.

Field hockey isn't weird! It's my dream!!!

Dream on, honey.

So it looks like you're going to have to do some observing on your own. This is terrible!!!

You'll be fine.

Field Hockey – DAY 1

I achieved my goals for the day! This wasn't too difficult, as my main goals were to stay on the team and not get hurt, not hurt anyone, and talk with Sukie, and I did all four!

I bask in the glow of your accomplishments. What did you and Sukie talk about?

She said

because she wanted me to pass her the ball. I tried, but Deirdre intercepted it and then Coach Tkaczuk shouted at me for not being more aggressive. Then, when Daddy came to pick me up Sukie asked, "Is that your dad?" and I said, "Yes."

I wish I was on the field hockey team. Guru Taralanna says I'm very aggressive.

Yesterday after practice while we were waiting for our parents to pick us up, Sukie and I had an entire conversation!

You're kidding me! What did she say?

She was asking about Daddy and Papa Dad, and then she told me that she would love to have two fathers. She doesn't have any.

Neither do I! Not really, anyway. Did you tell her that I don't have any fathers?

Yes, but there's more. I'll tell you after school, I think that Ms. Mulligan just saw us passing this note.

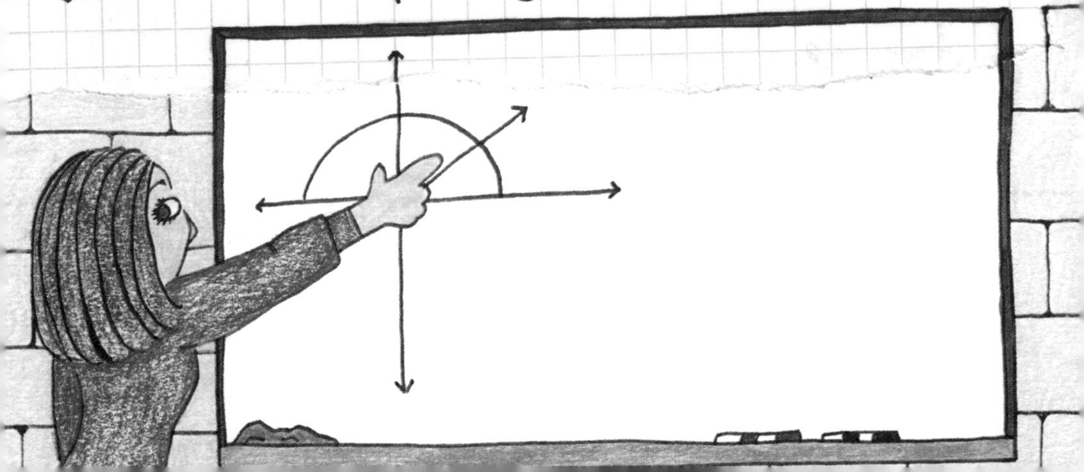

Sukie's Mystery

Sukie told me that her father died when she was really little, and now her mother is sick. Her aunt has lots of money and sends cars to pick Sukie up after school.

I was hoping that her secret would be that she was a secret agent or something.

I don't even know how much of a secret it is. Everyone on the field hockey team seems to know about it. The Popular Girls know.

Is her mom going to be okay?

I don't know.

I wish it had been a happier secret.

Me too.

Sukie as a Secret Agent.

Much better.

Guess what I found out?

Field hockey practice makes you sore?

Oh wait, no, that's what I found out.

Jane doesn't like Roland!

So?

I overheard Jane tell Lisa in music class that she flirts with Roland because she has a crush on his brother Pete.

That's not very nice to Roland.

Why do you care?

I don't. It's just not very nice to be not nice.

You like Roland!

That looks nothing like me.

LEARN IMPROVE → Your drawing!

We have a PROBLEM.

It's not a problem.

Lydia has auditioned for the solo in Chorus.

Which I got. Jane didnt seem too happy about it, but she congratulated me after Gretchen did.

But it's the solo in Roland's song!!!

And now we are happy in our mutual assurances! And I am betraying my best friend by singing this stupid song! Tra la la la la la!!!

Nice drawing.

It's silly that Julie cares about whether or not I sing the solo—someone's going to sing it, so it might as well be someone who is good and respectful about it.

It's embarrassing to have a song written about you! Why can't you just pretend to be sick on the day of the concert so that it doesn't get played?

Julie needs to get over herself because I've worked so hard to get a solo and it's not even in English so no one will ever know it's about her.

I think that Lydia is too obsessed with her fathead solo to see how mean she's being to me.

I think that Julie needs to count to ten and realize she's being really selfish.

1ST Field Hockey Game

Papa Dad came and took a million billion totally embarrassing pictures.

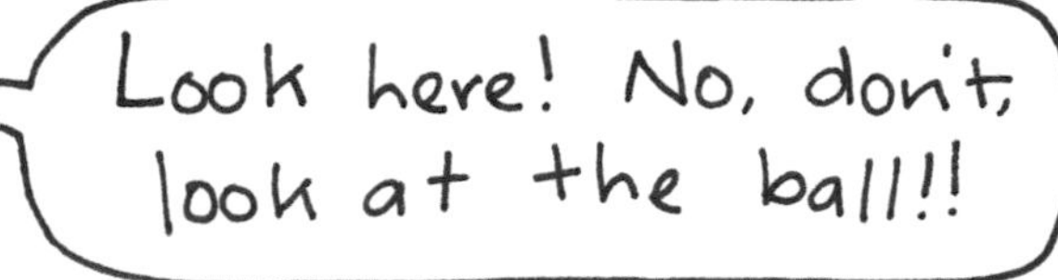

Look here! No, don't, look at the ball!!

I don't know if I'll want to see the pictures because we lost the game. The Field Hockey Girls DO NOT LIKE LOSING. I was a little disappointed, but Maxine was really upset. I was a little scared to sit next to her.

This cannot and will not happen again.

Okay.

After the game Sukie was waiting for her driver to pick her up, and Papa Dad offered to give her a ride home. At first she looked like she was going to say no, but Papa Dad hinted that there would be an ice-cream stop, so she called her aunt's driver to tell him not to come. We had a good time. Papa Dad was super embarrassing, but Sukie thought he was funny so I guess it was okay.

Gretchen invited me to come to her house for a sleepover!!!

I'm still mad at you.

Don't be mad, don't you see that Gretchen is impressed with me for getting the solo? That's why I got the invite! This is the whole reason that we've been working on the Handbook!

I guess it's kind of exciting.

I'm going to take so many notes and tell you everything that happens! This is going to be great!!!

Aren't you nervous that something bad will happen?

No, I'm too excited!

...Like what?

Things that could go HORRIBLY WRONG during a Sleepover

Allergic Reaction

Stepping on Someone's head while going to the bathroom

Really bad outburst brought on by extreme nervousness

I've been observing you all in an attempt to gain popularity!

Sleepover Observations

by Lydia

Gretchen's house is huge! And the lawn is huge! And she has four dogs and they're all really small!

Lisa and Jane were there, but Sukie wasn't. They said that she was going to come but that her family needed her. I didn't tell them that I knew about Sukie's mom already. That would have been weird.

Gretchen, Jane, and I slept on the floor. Lisa slept on the couch. She said that she always needs to sleep on a soft surface.

She could have slept on the dogs.

I didn't have any allergic reactions (we had pizza for dinner), and I made sure to go to the bathroom before we got into our sleeping bags, but there was one weird moment

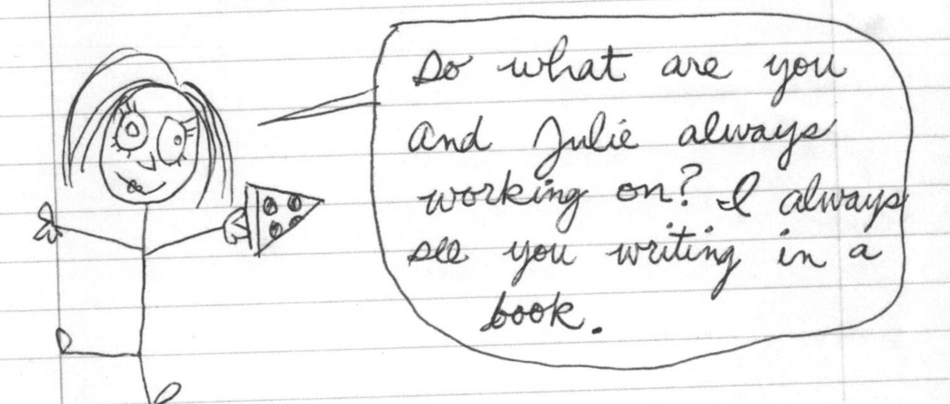

So what are you and Julie always working on? I always see you writing in a book.

I told her that we knew twin sisters named Chloe and Zoe and that they lived in New York City and we were making a scrapbook for them.

But here's something interesting that I learned - did you know that Gretchen's older sister Birgit used to be sort of friends with Melody?

The Story of BIRGIT and MELODY

Do you remember when my parents were getting divorced?

Sure, you were over at my house practically every day. That's when Daddy and Papa Dad started calling you their other daughter and they got us Bad Cat.

All that time Melody was over at Gretchen and Birgit's house! But that was before...

THE ILL-FATED TRIP TO BUCK's VALLEY

Birgit and Melody must have had a fight, because Birgit decided to steal all of Melody's socks and underwear.

Eww. Who would want someone else's underwear?

Birgit wouldn't tell Melody where her stuff was, and Melody had to spend the rest of the trip wearing the same dirty underwear and socks, and everyone in the school started calling her Smelly Melly. And Birgit still calls her Smelly Melly.

Gretchen's sister seems really mean.

Yeah. Still, we shouldn't be judged by our family members.

May

Sukie wasn't at practice today. Coach Tkaczuk said that her mother wasn't doing well, and we all made Sukie a card. I drew the picture on the front, and all of the field hockey girls liked it.

I don't think that it will stop them from knocking me around during practice, but they knock everyone around during practice, so I don't take it personally.

And they always help me up afterward and slap me on the back (which is sometimes worse than being knocked over).

Dee liked my drawing so much that she asked if I would help to make posters for her campaign to be elected President of the 6th grade class for next year!!

You like? *I think we have a problem.*

GRETCHEN vs. DEE

Not good.

Pretty bad.

Gretchen is running for President too!!!

Every one is talking about how much they love my posters! Dee is really thrilled.

They might be a little too good. Lisa told me during music class that Gretchen might not get elected because of your posters. Maybe you could make some for Gretchen, too?

That would be weird. Dee is my friend. And she can knock me down really easily. I don't want to make her mad.

But if Dee wins, that will ruin all the hard work we did to be friends with the Popular Girls!

I thought we were trying to BE the Popular Girls, not to BE FRIENDS WITH the Popular Girls.

It's the same thing.

I don't think it is.

You

a tomato

Just because you are next to a tomato doesn't make you a tomato.

???

It makes sense in my brain.

The art teacher, Mr. Rappaport, told me that my campaign posters were great! He wants me to help design posters for other occasions, like during Parent/Teacher Conference Day, and Valentine's Day, and Culturefest. I've been working on all sorts of sketches and when it comes time to make the posters, you could help me!

If you're such a great artist, you don't need my help.

I just thought it would be fun.

For you, maybe. Gretchen's sister said she would make some posters on the computer. That's easier, and we won't get so messy.

I don't get that messy.

Where were you yesterday after school? I called you, but your sister said you weren't home.

Lisa's mom picked her up from school and offered me a ride home. We stopped at her house first and hung out.

Why didn't you call me?

I couldn't use the Ladybug in front of Lisa!

I guess not. What's Lisa's house like?

There's no clutter anywhere! Everything is very clean. The sofa was not that comfortable and I was a little afraid to touch anything, even in Lisa's room.

Next time go to the bathroom and call me from there!

I have breached the inner sanctum! I repeat, I have breached the inner sanctum!

Would I ever talk like that?

You would if you had called me.

NEW THINGS LEARNED FROM LISA

Chuck Cavelleri is a loser!

What do you mean?

Mike thinks that he's a loser, and the Popular Girls think he's ugly and stupid.

But you think Mike is a loser, so doesn't that make Chuck cool?

You don't understand anything. Chuck is lame.

I thought you liked him.

That's before I knew he was lame.

Boys are confusing.

Today I was in the grocery store with Papa Dad, and I saw Chuck with his mom, and he talked to me!

Have you seen Lydia? She missed class the other day.

That was the day that Jane and I stayed after school to help Gretchen hang her campaign posters. I guess I forgot to go to class.

It was so embarrassing! Afterward Papa Dad was all, "Ooooh, who's this Chuck? Does Roland know?" But I think Chuck really likes you.

Ewww! I wish I had never taken stick-fighting. I could have taken private voice lessons instead, like Jane does.

I thought you wanted to do Field Hockey.

No way, we hate the field hockey team! Except for you and Sukie, of course.

SHOCKING THINGS I LEARNED ABOUT DEIRDRE NUTTER

1. She's Dyslexic. She can't tell left from right without thinking about it first. Jane has seen her think about it before.

So?

2. If Deirdre were elected president, she'd only do what the field hockey team wants, not what would be good for the whole 6th grade class. Gretchen is Totally prepared to lead everyone, not just the little bit of the school that plays field hockey.

That's not true!

3. Deirdre has a Confusing and difficult-to-pronounce first name.

4. Gretchen doesn't need fancy posters to make herself look better, because everyone knows she's just better anyway.

We'll see about that.

Yet Another! **OBSERVATION:**

Lisa has become veeeerrrry interested in our conversations.

She asks about what we do when we hang out all the time.

If she's so interested, she could just ask me to come over her house. I would like to see the very extra clean house.

I just think she's keeping an eye on us because she's afraid I might be giving you election strategy secrets.

That's ridiculous, you guys aren't even winning.

Yes we are! Mostly. But we have to be careful anyway, because we don't want Lisa to find out about the Handbook.

Blah Blah Lisa!!
Lisa Lisa Lisa Blah Blah we're being loud!

OUR PLAN

In order to ensure that our private conversations remain private, particularly conversations about our "research," we have developed a method of verbal communication that cannot be overheard. We're going to talk in the bathroom. And we're going to continuously flush the toilet while we talk so no one can accidentally overhear. Brilliant!

Just a week later!

I can't sit with you at lunch today— Gretchen wants me to sit with them.

Why can't we both sit with them?

I didn't ask. But I will when I sit with them and then maybe you can sit with us tomorrow.

But who am I going to sit with today?

During lunch Lisa started asking me about your mom.

Why?

I think that she wanted me to tell her about Daddy and Papa Dad.

I thought that everyone already knew about my dads. I told her about them when we were at Buck's Valley.

But she made it sound like having two fathers and no mom was bad.

What did she say?

She said that it was no wonder you dress so badly because you don't have a mom to buy you clothes.

What's wrong with the way I dress?

Maybe you shouldn't wear overalls so much.

But they're comfortable! What else did she say?

She started to say that she felt sorry for you because your family isn't normal, and Sukie told her to shut up!!!

Wow! What did you say?

I was too shocked to say anything! Let's go to the bathroom to talk.

We were talking in the bathroom until we were interrupted by Ms. Mulligan

Are you girls feeling okay?
Do your tummies hurt?
Yes.
No.
Because you've been flushing the toilet a lot lately. A Lot. I think you should go to see The Nurse.

So we went to the nurse's office. The Nurse sat us down in front of one of the private examination areas while she tried to get half an orange crayon out of Jamie Burke's nose.

Then *this* happened...

I don't know how anyone would want to be friends with Lisa. She's never, ever happy or friendly.

You're right. But Gretchen and Jane and Sukie like her and I like them, so maybe there's something more to her?

The only reason anyone likes her is because she's rich and she buys her friendships.

Ha! Her mom probably pays Gretchen and Jane and Sukie to hang out with her.

And then, while we were laughing, **LISA** came out from behind the screen at The Nurse's office!!!

Do you think she knew that we were talking about her?

No, she thought we were talking about someone else named Lisa whose parents are really rich and is friends with totally different girls named Gretchen and Jane and Sukie.

What are we going to do?

Other than feel horribly ashamed?

WHAT ARE WE GOING TO DO?

We should apologize.

No, we should not! If we apologize it's like we're admitting we did something wrong.

We did do Something wrong! We said mean, mean, hurtful things!

We don't even know for sure that she heard what we said. She hasn't mentioned it to anyone. Let's pretend it didn't happen and everything will be fine. Besides, she didn't say very nice things about you.

Two wrongs do not make a right.

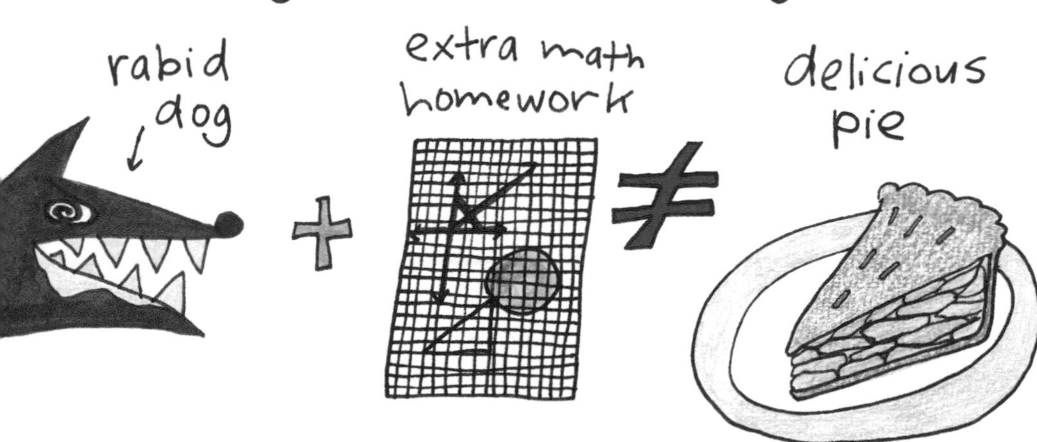

We can tell Lisa that it was Opposite Day, and we were saying things that are the opposite of what we'd normally say!

If it were Opposite Day, I wouldn't be wearing overalls. Or I'd be wearing them on my head.

We could tell her that we were rehearsing for a play we wrote.

Do you think she'd like us writing a play about a character named "Lisa" who only has friends because she buys them?

Okay, we'll tell her that you are very poor and that you're jealous of her for being rich and having a mom.

We could also tell her that you are possessed by aliens who have beamed down to Earth to ruin your social life.

Do you think she'd believe it?

Probably just as much as she'd believe we're playwrights on Opposite Day who don't have any money. Let's just

APOLOGIZE.

We need Outside Advice.

If you've said something hurtful, you should apologize.

So there.

I'm getting a second opinion.

Duh Nile ain't just a river in Egypt.

I have no idea what that means.

Maybe she's been working on a report on North Africa or something.

Last night I had a dream that Melody and I were on a boat floating down the Nile and Lisa was in a bigger boat pushing us into the mouth of an alligator that also looked like Lisa!!!

You need to stop listening to weird things that you hear from Smelly Melly. Just chill and everything will be fine.

So we've decided to pretend like nothing happened, even though it did and I'm not feeling too proud of myself.

Tomorrow night is the Spring Concert! Roland says my Norwegian accent is coming along very well.

Papa Dad and Daddy are planning to sit next to the Asbjørnsens. They call them "Matilda" and "Thor" when they talk with them on the phone.

Papa Dad wants us to dress in traditional Norwegian garb, but Daddy refuses, thank goodness.

I CAN'T BELIEVE SHE DID IT!!

LYDIA TOLD THE WHOLE SCHOOL THAT THE SONG WAS ABOUT ME!

She said that Lisa dared her to, so she had to do it.

I dare you to betray your BEST FRIEND in the whole entire world.

okay!

And this is a Norwegian Love Song written by Roland Asbjørnsen for his inspiration, JULIE GRAHAM-CHANG.
I HATE HER.

Lydia's been calling and calling. I am not going to talk to her EVER AGAIN. Daddy and Papa Dad have their worried faces on. Daddy made a suggestion:

Why don't you write Lydia a note telling her how you feel?

I hate her.

I know.

Oof, you're getting big for this.

Papa Dad suggested that we move to Guam to avoid Lydia, but I don't think he was being serious.

Julie, please don't be mad. Like I told you, I didn't mean to make you feel bad. If it's any consolation, Gretchen asked me why I decided to talk about the song before I sang the solo. I told her that you didn't mind, but I think she knows that you actually did mind, and now she's not really talking to me when I sit with them at lunch.

Please, let's just forget about it, okay? I found out that Jane secretly doesn't like Lisa either—she told me. Give me a call and I'll tell you all about it.

MY GREAT BIG LIST ABOUT WHY LYDIA WAS A BAD FRIEND

Note I write "was" instead of "is" because she "was" my friend and now she "is" not.

1. Lydia wasn't satisfied with having one really good friend, and worked really, really hard to get more. Lydia is greedy.
2. Lydia made her one really good friend help her to get new friends. Lydia is bossy.
3. Lydia figured that her one really good friend would always be a really good friend no matter what she did or said, even if she did really mean things. Lydia is stupid.
4. Lydia promised to learn how to knit, and now her one really good friend disappointed her dad because Lydia is lazy.
5. Lydia never cared about anyone but herself. Lydia is selfish.

Okay, you know what? I apologized. I said I was sorry and I meant it, but **YOU ARE TOO SENSITIVE!!** So what if I told the whole school that Roland likes you? **WHO CARES?**

I know you don't like the attention, but at least I never called you **GREEDY** and **BOSSY** and **STUPID** and **LAZY** and **SELFISH.**

THAT'S MEAN.

Maybe I should have been more sensitive, but you need to **GET OVER IT** because if you can't accept an apology, I don't want to be friends with you!!!

So call me.

Oh no, someone likes me and other people know about it! It's the end of the world! Boo and hoo!

If you don't keep this book this time, I'm going to throw it out. Or maybe I'll give it to Gretchen, how would you like that?

Yesterday Gretchen asked me why I wasn't hanging out with Julie anymore, and I told her it was because Julie really wants Deirdre to win the election, so she's decided not to hang out with me anymore because I am friends with her (Gretchen). I thought that Gretchen would be pleased to know how loyal I was, but she said

That's terrible! I didn't think that Julie was like that!

I'd rather not be president at all if it separates two good friends!

Well, Julie's really competitive. You know how those Field Hockey girls are.

And then I remembered that Sukie was on the team and I felt even worse. Luckily Gretchen didn't mention it again.

Gretchen's sister only sort of helped us with the posters on the computer. I don't know if they're going to do the trick.

Vote 4 Gretchen

4

PREZ

Julie refuses to take the book or talk to me. This is stupid. We've been friends since we were babies.

And now she spends all her time with Dee and the field Hockey Girls. I saw them making fun of Julie for being Roland's love interest and she just laughed it off. This is a double standard!

INJUSTICE!!

She can't still be mad at me.

Yesterday the Field Hockey team won a big-deal game and today everyone was just congratulating them and acting like they won the Academy Award for field hockey or something.

And I saw Mike Cavelleri talking to **JULIE!**

Good job, Jules!

Why, thank you Mike. I'm going to smile and flirt with you even though you are Lydia's mortal enemy who tortured her for years!!

I wanted to tell her "Good job" but I didn't. Maybe I should have.

Today Gretchen started asking me about my friends in New York, **Chloe** and **Zoe**. She said that her mother has a sister in New York and they might go there to visit them if I don't mind. I didnt know what to say, so I just started making stuff up.

Chloe and Zoe live really close to the Statue of Liberty and they're never around during the summer because their parents send them to Switzerland because they get tired of all the tourists crowding around their house when they're in line to see the Statue of Liberty.

I don't know if Gretchen believed me. I hope she did. I don't think she did.

OBSERVATION

Lisa and Gretchen slept over at Jane's house last night and I wasn't invited. Jane said that they thought I was busy with my stick-fighting class, but it's not like I couldn't have come over afterward.

I HATE ESKRIMA!

We are having piles of fun!
sticks!

Gretchen, Lisa, and Jane spent their lunch hour passing out Gretchen's campaign stickers, and they didn't ask me if I wanted to help them. I was going to just join them but I felt weird about it.

I sat with the Field Hockey Girls instead. Julie ignored me. Dee was nice enough, but it wasn't the same as having a real group of friends that really want me to be there. Dee was just being polite. I think that she'll actually make a good 6th grade Class President. I was going to offer to help her with her campaign, but I think that will make everyone feel awkward.

It's funny, they don't say anything but I can tell how they feel. I wish they liked me more. I should have been observing them this whole time.

The election is next week! There are posters all over the school. And now there's a third candidate! Jamie Burke is running. Maybe if he wins, Julie and I will be friends again.

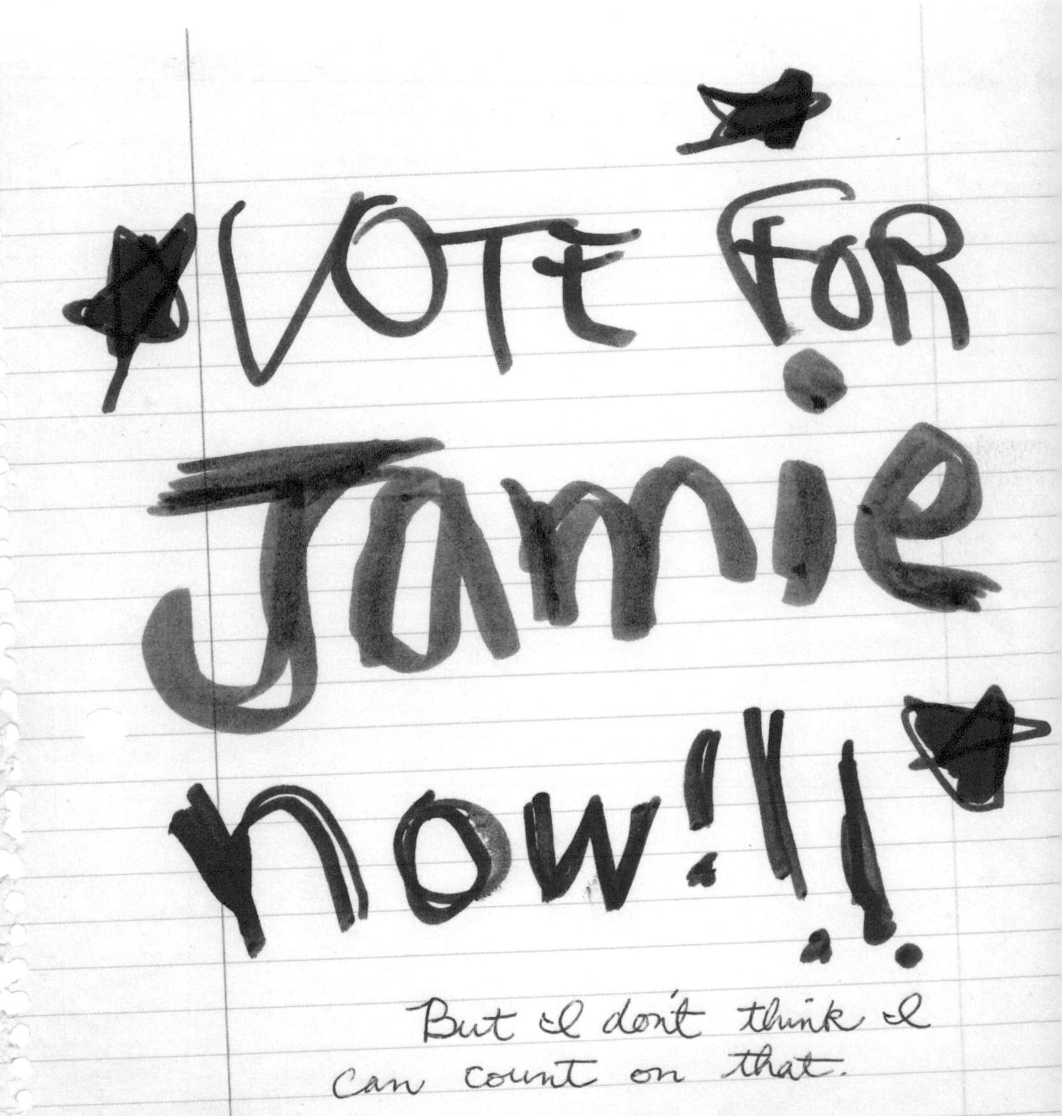

But I don't think I can count on that.

Melody taught me how to knit. Who knew that Melody knew how to knit??? She said that knitting was really "counterculture." I don't know what that means, but look what I made!

It's not perfect, but I'm learning.

It's a lot easier to learn when someone shows you how to do it. If Julie would talk to me, I could show her how to knit and she could make that sweater for Papa Dad. I wish she'd stop not being friends with me.

DEE WON THE ELECTION!

It's no wonder, really, Dee's signs and stickers were so much cooler.

Vote
4
Gretchen

GRETCHEN
is
GREAT

I should have congratulated her and Julie, but they were so surrounded by people congratulating them, and I didn't want to get lost in the crowd.

Come to the
VERY FIRST MEETING
of
The
ART CLUB!
Sign up outside of
Mr. Rappaport's
classroom
Julie has posters all over the school advertising a new Art Club. If I hadn't encouraged her to be on the Field Hockey Team, she would have never gotten so popular.

LISA HAS SIGNED UP TO JOIN THE ART CLUB!

I saw her name right up there on the sign-up sheet outside of the art room!

And I saw Lisa talking with Julie about it at lunch! She came up to the Field Hockey Table! I was eating lunch with Roland. I asked him what he thought about it and he said,

Julie is nice and smart! Why wouldn't anyone want to be friends with her? Even though she is short.

She isn't really that short. People in Norway must be gigantic.

Melody showed me how to purl today. Purling is basically like knitting but backwards—that's what she says, anyway. To me it seemed like a completely different kind of stitch, but once I learned how to do it, I could make this!

It's called a "ribbing"

Melody's not so bad. She and Roland are really the only people who talk to me now. You'd think he'd be mad at me, but he's not. I think that Julie is avoiding him, too. Melody says

Misery loves company.

Although I don't think that Melody or Roland are miserable.

Not like me.

I was starting to feel like no one was ever going to talk with me again besides Melody, Roland, and the Cheerful Librarian.

And where is your little friend? The one who likes wearing overalls?

But I saw Chuck at the library. He was reading books about comic books and he showed them to me and asked if I was going to take Eskrima again. I told him I didn't know, but I might if he does.

Now I feel so bad about calling him lame. I almost apologized but decided it would be better if he never knew that I used to think he was a loser.

Today I hung out with Chuck at the library again. He seems to spend a lot of time there (and I guess I do too, because it's better than answering a million and one questions from my mom about Julie).

Why don't you call Julie? I can't have both you and Melody moping around all day.

Chuck asked why I wasn't hanging out with Julie anymore, and before I could stop myself I told him the whole story (leaving out the part where I thought he was lame).

OBSERVATIONS

1. Julie still isn't talking to me.
2. I am still not talking to Julie.
3. If Julie continues to not talk to me, and I continue to not talk to Julie, we're **NEVER GOING TO TALK TO EACH OTHER EVER AGAIN.**

I told Chuck about my observations and he suggested that if maybe I talk to Julie, and apologize, my #3 observation might not happen. He's pretty smart. It's probably because he's older. I don't get why he's not more popular, although he doesn't really seem to care.

CHUCK CAVELLERI's rules for HAPPINESS

1. Do what makes you happy.

Chuck likes Eskrima and Comic books, so he takes classes with Guru Taralanna and Collects comics.

2. Hang out with other people who make you happy.

Chuck spends most of his time with the Eskrima guys. They never seem to worry about how unpopular they are. It's weird but also nice.

I am talking about stuff that Lydia doesn't understand, but I am happy.

I tried to think about what makes Julie happy. She likes to draw and make art and hang out with her dads and play with Bad Cat and hang out with me (or at least she used to). Now I feel like I made her try to do things that didn't make her happy. But I did make her try out for the field hockey team, and that makes her happy. So trying new things can't be that bad.

Then I tried to think about what makes me happy. I like singing and being onstage and I like hanging out with Julie (although I don't always like playing with Bad Cat). And even though it was exciting to sleep over at Gretchen's house, I didn't like the way that her sister acted. And Lisa's house was scary clean. I miss Julie. Chuck is right. I have to talk to her.

PLACES to TALK to JULIE

1. Julie's House. <u>Problem:</u> she might not be home, and then I might have to talk with Daddy and Papa Dad, and if they're as mad at me as she is, I don't think I could take it

How dare you come to our home! We don't like you! Go away forever!!!

2. A field hockey game.

<u>Problem:</u> she'd probably be pretty busy, playing field hockey.

Let's talk!

3. ART CLUB

Problem: I am terrible at art!

Examples of me being terrible at art can be seen Whenever I Draw Anything.

I talked to Melody because she's good at art. Well, she dresses weird so I figure she's good at art. I showed her some of my drawings and she was less than impressed.

Primitive.

Then Melody showed me how I actually am sort of an artist. Chuck thinks I'm artistic. So tomorrow I'm going to take my art to the art club and talk to Julie. I hope she accepts my art. And my apology.

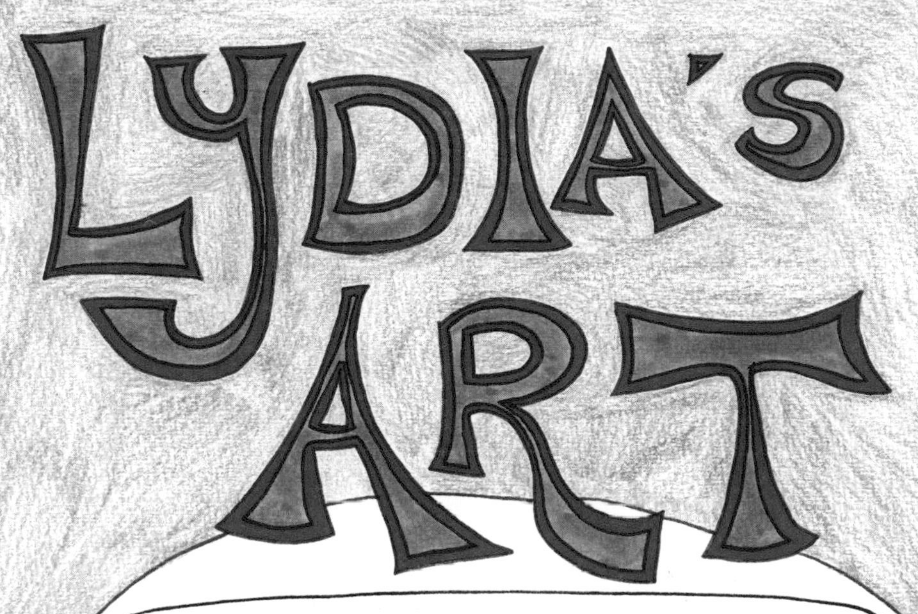
LYDIA'S
ART

I am so sorry that I've been a bad friend

Lydia made a scarf for Papa Dad!

Papa Dad loooooooves his new scarf! He wore it even though the weather was really warm.
You really don't have to wear it right now.
But I look so good!
Daddy says you're going to dehydrate.

THINGS I'VE LEARNED OVER THE PAST FEW WEEKS

1. How to play Mancala
2. Playing Mancala ALL THE TIME gets kind of old.
3. Laughing at myself is good. Dee and the Field Hockey Girls made so much fun of me for being Roland's "girlfriend" but they weren't being mean, and I kind of felt silly about being so embarrassed.

When you marry Roland, can we visit you in Norway?

What's Norwegian for smooooch?

4. Even though I had friends, I still missed writing notes and talking with Lydia, because I never have to explain jokes to her.

Because I'm super-smart? Suuure.

5. I learned that no one ever really thought of us as "unpopular." They just didn't know we existed.

6. Lisa's actually not that bad. She's just always worried about what other people think about her. She's a lot more relaxed when she's making something out of clay.

She's good at it too.

7. I learned that there are worse things in life than boys liking you.

8. Being mean just makes me feel worse.

9. And when someone apologizes and really means it, you should accept it.

Gretchen came up to me after class and asked if I wanted to sleep over her house tonight.

Are you going?

I told her I wasn't missing Burrito Night at the Graham-Chang house. She said that you could come too.

Maybe I will.

Next time.

When it's Chopped Liver Night.

So Melody (!!) helped Lydia teach me how to purl. She seemed kind of happy to see me.

Hey. You're back.

Or as happy as Melody ever seems. But she's a good teacher. I asked her how she learned, and she told us that she hangs out at the yarn store!

Weird, right? I never knew. I thought she just stayed in her room, being angry at the world.

Me too.

I told her that it was funny to think of her hanging out with a bunch of old-lady knitters, and then Melody said something kind of neat:

COOLEST PEOPLE WE KNOW

Sukie

Chuck

Melody

Dee

Roland

Bad Cat

US!

Acknowledgments

I would like to thank the New York, New Jersey, and Texas Ignatows; Stephen Barr at Writers House; Scott Auerbach, Howard Reeves, Susan Van Metre, Melissa Arnst, and Chad Beckerman at Amulet Books; Maggie Lehrman, my fantastic editor, whose enthusiasm for Lydia and Julie is matched only by her mix-making skills; Chuck Wyatt, for his invaluable knowledge of Eskrima; The Harem of the Dancing Fisherman, for sharing their expertise in the fiber arts; Rich Harrington, Bill Brown, and the Illustration Department at Moore College of Art, for continuing to teach me long after my student days had ended; Dan Lazar, my amazing, resilient agent at Writers House, who answered my emails at all hours, told me it was okay for me wear sneakers to meetings, and never gave up on me, and without whom this book would never have come into being; and Richard Ignatow, whose ranting tirades about the latest news story on NPR cannot hide the most supportive, patient, greatest dad a cartoonist could ask for. I am most thankful for the love and encouragement of my wonderful husband, Mark, my best friend.

About the Author

Amy Ignatow is an illustrator and teacher who has also been a farmer, a florist, a short-order vegan cook, a dancing chicken, an SAT prep instructor, a telefundraiser, a wedding singer, a ghostwriter for Internet personal ads, a reporter, and an air-brush face and body painter working under the name "Ooga." She graduated from Moore College of Art and Design and lives in Philadelphia with her husband, Mark, and their cat, Mathilda, whom they believe to be well-meaning despite all evidence to the contrary.

To my friends, who are the coolest people I know.
—Ig

Artist's Note: The materials used to create the book are ink, colored pencil, colored marker, yarn, and digital.

PUBLISHER'S NOTE: This is a work of fiction. Names, characters, places, and incidents are either the product of the author's imagination or are used fictitiously, and any resemblance to actual persons, living or dead, business establishments, events, or locales is entirely coincidental.

Cataloging-in-Publication Data has been applied for and may be obtained from the Library of Congress.
ISBN 978-0-8109-8421-9

Text and illustrations copyright © 2010 Amy Ignatow
Book design by Amy Ignatow and Melissa Arnst

Published in 2010 by Amulet Books, an imprint of ABRAMS. All rights reserved. No portion of this book may be reproduced, stored in a retrieval system, or transmitted in any form or by any means, mechanical, electronic, photocopying, recording, or otherwise, without written permission from the publisher. Amulet Books and Amulet Paperbacks are registered trademarks of Harry N. Abrams, Inc.

Printed and bound in China
10 9 8 7 6 5 4 3 2 1

Amulet Books are available at special discounts when purchased in quantity for premiums and promotions as well as fundraising or educational use. Special editions can also be created to specification. For details, contact specialmarkets@abramsbooks.com or the address below.

ABRAMS
THE ART OF BOOKS SINCE 1949
115 West 18th Street
New York, NY 10011
www.abramsbooks.com